I Have No Idea
What I'm Doing

stories by
andrew wayne adams

ERASERHEAD PRESS
PORTLAND, OREGON

ERASERHEAD PRESS
P.O. BOX 10065
PORTLAND, OR 97296

www.eraserheadpress.com
facebook/eraserheadpress

ISBN: 978-1-62105-262-3
Copyright © 2018 by Andrew Wayne Adams
Cover art copyright © 2018 Hauke Vagt

Printed in the USA.

For Sam Reeve

CONTENTS

a sHarp Girl

I am a biochemistry major working on her doctorate and halfway through a test I get up to sharpen my pencil. The sharpener (one of those antiquated hand-cranked ones) is as large as a sewing machine. Its guts chuckle as I stick my pencil in and turn the handle. Its casing, made of turtle shell, glistens with a film of pond water that never evaporates. I sharpen my pencil for fifteen minutes, the shriek and grind of it disturbing the class worse than a jackhammer. A few students kill themselves because damn, they just can't take it, and driblets of blood spurt from their slit wrists onto their tests, into the answer blanks, which will probably cause the professor to suspect cheating when she sees the matching responses. But we could use a little scandal.

Finally I finish tormenting everyone, figuring my pencil is probably sharp enough to artificially inseminate an egg, which is how I like it. But when I inspect the tool, what I find is a hollow wooden tube, the stick of graphite or lead or whatever vanished from its center. The most important part of the pencil—its heart, its brain, its sex organ—gone! I screw my eye to the hole in the pencil sharpener, peer in at the dark and silent machinery. I am an experimental physics major working on her doctorate and I need that graphite core to complete my test... won't resort to answering in blood like the others...

I shrink myself to the size of a pea (which I learned how to do as an undergrad) and enter the pencil sharpener. A bed of ancient shavings fills the pit of the casing like shreds of withered bone, while overhead there looms a horrid octopus of cylinders threaded with disintegrating edges. Every surface gritty with coal-black dust, the air in here whooshes as if in a seashell.

Something moves in the mass grave of shavings, slithering with a hiss through those brittle flakes, and I see it: a long thin snake of black graphite. It raises its head at me, rearing up from the pit like a sea serpent. Actually, it could just as well be its ass as its head, since the snake is a featureless rod. It bends sinuously, not snapping as graphite should, as if its molecules have learned a new trick, and I wonder what other new tricks to look out for... if it might have a mouth full of teeth somewhere, or an emotional complex requiring delicate care...

I am a psychology major and I know delicate care, which is why I leap onto the snake's back and throttle its neck. Actually, it could just as well be its crotch as its neck. I throttle the snake's ass or its boobs or whatever, and I whisper in its ear, "You will return to me." I whisper in its nose, "I have a test to finish."

The graphite shoots forward in terror and bursts through the wall, out through the turtle-shell casing of the huge pencil sharpener. I cling to its back, riding it through the air like Atreyu riding Falkor in *The NeverEnding Story.* We arc across the room, toward where my test sits unfinished on a tiny desk, and our trajectory lands us perfectly on the test, where we skid to a stop, the stick of graphite laying down a jagged mark as we do so.

"Time!" shouts the professor through a bullhorn, and cracks a whip to threaten any student who doesn't immediately drop her pencil. The graphite serpent dies and rolls off the desk and shatters into Cantor dust.

I make myself big again and stare down at my test. My test with half the answers blank, just that crumbled scrawl slashing the page where the graphite kissed it like an arrow ill shot. The professor stands at the head of the class and sucks in all the tests with a giant vacuum, and I slit my wrists but stay alive long enough for the graded tests to come back a week later, walking around for a week with my arms elevated and pressure on the wounds, until I learn that I got a perfect score, the chance jag of graphite on page five being the only correct answer to the entire test.

I am a philosophy major working on her death and I clap my hands in glee and finally bleed out.

THE EARLY NORWEGIAN BLACK METAL SCENE

A year before they broke up, Mark took Terry to a party where no one knew each other. That was the point of the party, that no one knew each other. When Mark and Terry arrived, they had to split up and pretend to be strangers. Mark hid in the bushes while Terry went in first. Twenty minutes later, Mark followed. Both of them performed the same ritual of putting their coats in a bedroom at the end of a long hall and grabbing a bottle of craft beer from a giant tub full of ice and staking out spots along the wall in the main room. Their spots were next to the fish tank (Mark) and in front of the H. R. Giger print (Terry). A clownfish was drunk.

Eventually Mark approached Terry.

"Did you see that guy pour rum in the fish tank?" he said, and sipped his beer, which was chocolaty and strong.

"He said it was for the pirate," Terry said. There was a pirate figurine in the tank, next to a sunken ship with skeletons on it. "Because, you know, rum."

"Can I taste your beer?"

"Yeah. Tastes like cilantro, right?"

"Yeah," wiping his mouth, "and Korean barbecue sauce."

Terry looked around. "Do you know whose party this is?"

"No. I don't know anyone here."

"Me neither."

"What's your name?"

"Terry."

"Terry? I'm Mark."

A tall guy with nice shoes popped up beside them, convivially drunk and sure of his own standing. He said, "What a party, huh? I mean, what a concept. No one here knows each other. I'm Bob." Bob watched a new arrival (hot chick) walk past them toward the coat room. "Excuse me," he said, and walked toward the coat room with a hammer and duct tape.

Mark and Terry watched him go. They looked at each other and laughed at it all. They both had crazy laughs that sounded like they were choking on cartilage, or like their throats were blood motors. They laughed for six seconds.

Terry said, "Bob hasn't changed a bit since grade school, has he?"

Mark's face hardened. "You know him?"

Before Terry could answer, there was a commotion at the front door as the early Norwegian black metal scene crashed the party.

They came in all at once, a few dozen people squeezing as one through the doorframe—getting stuck at first, then exploding across the room like confetti as the clot broke. They landed all around: on the couch, by the fish tank, in front of the Alex Grey print, behind the TV, in the chip dip. They immediately found each other and pretended to be strangers.

Mark and Terry watched them for a while. Eventually Mark said, "These guys are full of it. They all know each other. Look how they're dressed. They're part of a gang or something. They're Juggalos."

"No, they're the early Norwegian black metal scene."

Mark's face hardened. "You know them?"

Before Terry could answer, one of the members of the early Norwegian black metal scene killed one of the other members, then with bloodstained hands took a sip of his beer that tasted like falafel as he moved away to look at the Gustave Doré print on the wall (that illustration from *Paradise Lost* of the angels falling out of heaven). A few people screamed at the murder and called the cops, who would be there in six seconds.

Mark said, "The cops'll shut this party down."

Terry said, "The cops'll get this party started."

The cops came and said, "We'll just take the perpetrator and be on our way, don't mind us, an invisible force for good, oh and guess we better outline this body in chalk, there we go, and collect some of this here forensic evidence, yes, that'll do, don't mind us, an invisible net, oh and guess we better take your statements, my goodness you're articulate, all right, thank you, bye bye."

Later in the night people started posing for pictures with the murder victim. The murder victim smiled at being popular. His chalk outline got rubbed away from too many people brushing against it. People were talking openly now about their shared memories from high school, the funny things they did last weekend.

Eventually Bob emerged from the coat room with gouges in his face from long fingernails. He approached Mark and Terry again with fresh beers for them. Mark took the wasabi beer and Terry took the tobacco one.

Terry said, "This tastes just like my first cigarette. Remember that, Bob? You gave me a Marlboro at Shane's house. I was afraid of death, and I lit the filter by mistake. End of story."

Bob was preparing to laugh, but Mark cut him off, erupting, "How dare you know Terry!" He splashed his wasabi beer into the scratches on Bob's face. "Terry of indeterminate sex, whom I have loved since the first paragraph!"

Terry said, "It's true, gendered pronouns have been

assiduously avoided when it comes to me."

Bob winced as the beer stung his wounds. His face melted like wax and ran from the bone, splashing down from his great height to splatter the niceness of his shoes. With his face gone, skull exposed, he looked just like Skeletor, who had been his hero since birth. Catching a glimpse of himself in the reflective plastic over a Hieronymus Bosch print, he smiled. "Excuse me," he said, and walked off to test out life as a hero.

Terry glowered at Mark and said, "I think we should go."

"I'll get our coats."

In the coat room, someone had burned down a church. Mark sifted through the coats on the bed and selected two at random. One was ripped denim, the other was an Oakland Raiders jacket.

"Here," he said to Terry when he returned, and handed over the denim. Terry put it on. Mark put on the Oakland Raiders jacket.

The cops came back, a whole squad of them trying to squeeze through the door as one—getting stuck at first, then exploding across the room like confetti as the clot broke. A cop landed in front of Mark and slapped handcuffs on him, the landing and the cuffing part of one fluid motion.

Apparently someone had called about another murder; someone had seen Bob walking around looking like Skeletor, and had assumed he was dead. "You match the description of the suspect," the cop told Mark, glancing at his afro (which was tight, tidy) and his Starter jacket with the Oakland Raiders logo on it.

The cops all wore black uniforms. Most of them had grabbed beers and were standing around sipping them. A few were talking to Bob, taking his statement about the murder. Mark saw Bob pointing at him. The cops nodded. Bob told a racist joke and flexed his right bicep.

The cops nodded.

As a skull, Bob was always grinning now.

"Okay, time to go to jail," the cop said to Mark.

They started to drag him off. He looked at Terry and mouthed a plea. He was ignorant then of their breakup a year later.

"Terry," he said, "you know me."

Looking around, Terry said, "No. I don't know anyone here."

Later that night, someone sacrificed a goat that was chained to a stake in the center of the room. Terry went home with a girl named Belphegor.

Serial Killer Fan Fiction

At age twelve Ann fell in love with a serial killer. The serial killer was her mailman. His name was Centipede Kennedy. She went out every morning to meet him. He gave her the mail—always the same: an envelope for her father, no postage on it—and winked at her. She blushed and smiled.

Marry me marry me marry me!

Centipede Kennedy was old. Probably in his sixties. Ann loved the silver of his hair. She loved the worn finish of his skin. The washboard of wrinkles in his forehead. The exploded capillaries.

Every morning when she came in from getting the mail, her father took the envelope and disappeared into the basement for half an hour. She watched TV and ate Caterpillar Crunch (her favorite breakfast cereal) and did the homework due that day, and then her father emerged from the basement and drove her to school.

Whenever she watched TV and ate Caterpillar Crunch, the only thing on TV was commercials for Caterpillar Crunch.

One day she heard a scream from the basement. She froze, a spoonful of Caterpillar Crunch (dripping, raised halfway to her mouth) in her left hand, a pencil (doing differential equations) in her right. She looked toward the door that led to the basement. The door was full of throwing knives.

Another scream.

On TV, a child actor was eating Caterpillar Crunch and smiling nervously. Then a sheet of static truncated the commercial. When the static cleared, Ann saw a high-angle view of her own basement. The footage was grainy and without sound. It showed her father, seated in a folding chair with his pants around his ankles. In one hand he held a crumpled letter—in the other, his erect penis. But he had stopped what he was doing, because something was happening to him.

His flesh wriggled, as if made of inchworms. The colors and shapes that comprised him were shifting, bending. The planes of his face broke apart, sliding over and under each other like tectonic plates, and his mouth was twisted open, trying to scream again; but the scream was caught inside, trapped in a cave-in of membranes and cartilage, and soon even his mouth had vanished, overridden by his drooping ear.

A new face emerged from the old. Ann recognized it immediately.

Centipede Kennedy.

The serial killer mailman looked a lot like her father, actually. Just older. He looked at the letter in his hand—the letter that he had delivered to Ann that morning; that Ann had delivered to her father; that her father had been reading with his pants around his ankles—and he let it fall to the floor, where a rat came out and grabbed it and took it back through a hole in the wall.

Then the basement windows broke open as armored policemen swung in, clubs raised and voices braying. Ann heard the uproar from below, the shouts and shattering glass, and she drew closer to the mute TV, watching the clubs rise and fall in time to the meaty thuds coming up through the floorboards.

The policemen wrapped Centipede Kennedy in chains. They put ten straightjackets on him. They tied his shoelaces together.

Ann wanted to cry.

Centipede Kennedy looked up to where the TV eye was watching. He winked at Ann. She blushed and smiled.

Love me love me love me!

The policemen took the serial killer mailman away. The TV went back to playing a Caterpillar Crunch commercial.

No one drove Ann to school that day.

She collected all the newspaper clippings about Centipede Kennedy and his crimes. She kept the clippings in a shoebox that she hid behind a loose brick in the wall above her bed at the orphanage. She read them every night.

Her favorite clipping detailed a murder committed in the late 1980s. It ran: "Kennedy stalked the supple young woman for several months before making his move. Finally his bloodlust took control, and on September 14, 1987—a Monday—he went to Home Depot and bought twenty feet of rope and a butane torch. He used a coupon. That night he unlawfully entered the home of the supple young woman and unlawfully tied her up with the rope and applied the butane torch to each of her teeth until every tooth had popped like a little ceramic balloon. Neighbors report hearing screams and feeling apathetic about it. After torturing her teeth, Kennedy moved on to her genitals. For a full exposé of the genital mutilation, see my book, *Centipede Kennedy: Modalities of Discourse,* coming soon from Viking/Semiotext(e). The genitals thus dispatched, Kennedy made quick business of the rest. He pushed a safety pin through the heart of the supple young woman, then left through the front door."

At age thirteen Ann masturbated for the first time. For erotic stimulus she used the book the reporter had written. The book was as thick as a volume of federal statutes; it detailed every murder with forensic precision. She pressed flowers in it and drew hearts in the margins.

There were stray cats at the orphanage, and when they died Ann liked to watch the maggots writhe in their eye sockets. She kept some of the maggots as pets and raised them to maturity. She liked to watch them metamorphose.

At age sixteen she wrote her first letter to Centipede Kennedy. It ran: "You might not remember me, but I love you. You used to bring my father letters with no postage on them. My father metamorphosed into you, and then the police came and arrested him/you. I was 12 at the time. I was the little girl with the harelip and alopecia. Remember me? I hope you do.

"I love the way you killed your first victim. I love how you inserted the knife at a 32-degree angle. In that book the reporter wrote about you, she says that the 32-degree angle had something to do with the freezing point of water, that you were making a statement using the symbolism of the Fahrenheit temperature scale. Is that true? What were you trying to say exactly? Sorry if I seem dense.

"I love the way you tortured your first victim before killing her. I love how you bisected her nipple with a razor blade in homage to the film *Lo squartatore di New York* (1982, dir. Lucio Fulci). The book says that's one of your favorite movies. I haven't seen it yet, but I want to.

"I love how you hissed like a snake at her and shook maracas at her and made an X on her face with electrical tape. I love how you..."

The letter went on like that for five pages. It concluded: "...and even though they gave you 500 life sentences, I still believe you'll get out someday, because I know that we're meant to be together."

Ann signed the letter with an X and put it in a plain envelope with no postage on it and gave the envelope to her contact, a courier rat who specialized in smuggling things in and out of prisons. She gave the rat some cheese as payment. The cheese was full of maggots.

She wrote hundreds of letters like that. Every letter spoke at length of one of the murders, because Ann wanted to show her appreciation of them. She spent her days in the orphanage library, picking through books on art and psychology and quantum physics and philosophy—inventing insights to nervously put forth in her letters, interpretations she hoped would arouse respect. She learned a lot and forgot it all and scrawled out her missives with abandon.

Her letters addressed the murders chronologically. Sometimes the dates were confusing. It seemed like Centipede Kennedy had been killing for longer than he'd been alive. Into the distant past and future. Ann struggled with the dream logic of it, sometimes forgetting which century she was in.

The headmistress at the orphanage hated Ann. She was a giant woman with a harelip. She liked to chase Ann with a butterfly net through the library stacks. Ann always hid in the dictionary.

The headmistress was a former child actress who had starred in Caterpillar Crunch commercials. She looked a lot like Ann, actually. Just older. Her wings were full of exploded capillaries.

One day the mailman (a silvery wrinkled rat) came with a letter for Ann. It ran: "Thank you, sweetheart, for all of the letters. A contact of mine from an adjacent space-time has agreed to publish them—as an epistolary novel—and says he expects the book to flourish (says his space-time is full of fanatics). The working title is *Centipede Kennedy: Totalities of Discord*. You'll get full royalties (once the transdimensional contracts are settled), which I only hope can make up for some of what I stole from you in your child actress days. It was wicked of me to exploit you like that, honeybunch. *Forgive me forgive me forgive me!*

"I have to go soon. I hear the Shepard tone outside my cell, signaling lights out. Tonight is the night. The wormhole is here and I have my ticket. My face has changed again, both younger and older now. I have my mailbag full of your letters. Time to play my part—to go back and give myself the future.

"Daddy loves you, munchkin. Your mother was a cruel giantess. She was my mother too. Look out behind you."

Ann dropped the letter and looked out behind her. The headmistress was there. Ann dodged the swipe of her butterfly net. The headmistress grew two feet. She chased Ann through the library stacks. She was taller than the highest shelf. Ann could not find the dictionary to hide in. She ran deep into the stacks, pushing through cobwebs and toppled books, into a place of teetering disarray. Down gyres too constricted for the minotaur to follow.

The minotaur roared. The library shook.

Ann circulated into an unknown annex; then into an annex of the annex; then an annex of that... spiraling in or out along some segmented structure through the earth... rising and falling in fugal modulation...

All the books here were biblical fan fiction bound in human skin.

She wandered lost for forty days. To stay alive she trapped and ate stray cats. She ate maggots and caterpillars. Long blind worms and centipedes.

One day a rat led her home.

She stalked the rat because she wanted to eat it. The rat wanted to live, so it fled down gyres too constricted for

Ann to follow. Ann swung her butterfly net at it. She sent throwing knives after it. She roared.

The library shook.

Books fell like a snowstorm. Through the flurry, Ann saw the rat. She chased it. It was a flash of silver in the blizzard of books. She constricted her focus to that flash of silver, pursued it like a cat.

She lost it. Blowing books were all she saw. Like a wraparound sheet of static. A solid knit of bodiless wings.

The static cleared, and Ann was in the basement of her childhood home.

Police tape crisscrossed the space like a clownish spider web. Everything was as it had been. Glass on the floor from the broken windows. The folding chair in the center of the room, where her father had sat masturbating. Streaks of dried blood from when the policemen beat him.

Ann saw the rat. It scurried through a hole in the wall.

She dove at it.

The hole vomited a wave of crumpled paper. The wave hit Ann, covering her in paper cuts. Her blood sprinkled the pages. She picked one up.

It was a letter. One that she had written to Centipede Kennedy. All of her hundreds of letters were here, each one a complete blueprint for a murder. They had traveled back with Centipede Kennedy through the wormhole, and he had fed them to her father one at a time—her father, who charged them with fantasy, then realized them—rendering the future with utter fidelity.

And this rat had gathered every spent letter, making a nest of them in its hole. Archivist. Many of the letters were gnawed upon, ragged, as if the rat had thought they smelled of ripe cheese.

Ann sifted through the letters, looking for food.

She found a letter written on a stone tablet. It was not one of hers. It told of a murder yet to occur.

Ann lifted her gaze to the high corner of the basement. There was an eyeball there, mounted to the wall. A huge wet globe like the eye of a bull. It was a camera. Someone was watching. Ann hoped she knew who it was.

"I love you!" she screamed, although she knew the footage was mute.

In her hands, the stone tablet bubbled and warped. The etched words lifted from the stone, wriggling across it like inchworms. Like caterpillars.

Smiling into the camera, she ate the words one by one... consuming the genes of that final future murder...

The shadow of the rat rose up behind her.

ANALYSIS OF THE ANALYSIS
OF THE BREAKTHROUGH

The giant cockroach wears a Sigmund Freud mask.

"Tell me about your mother," the cockroach says.

I lie on the couch, one hand slid inside my shirt to hold my belly button. "My mother? She was a saint. An angel. Pure as porcelain."

The cockroach drags its chair close. Uncomfortably close. It says, "Tell me about your father."

I say, "Quit with the mind games, Dad."

My dad twitches his antennae and says, "I'm only trying to help you with your problem. To realize your full potential." He straightens his tie.

"I don't have a problem," I say.

"You can't achieve an erection," he says.

"Not true. I achieved one yesterday. At school. During an oral presentation."

"Look, I know it's hard, your father being your psychoanalyst. But you must be straight with me if you wish to overcome this trouble with your genitals." He pauses to light a cigar. The cigar is five feet long, two feet in diameter. "Now," he says, blowing smoke through the mouth-hole of his Freud mask. "Tell me about your father."

I sigh. "I'm a middle child. The two-hundred-thousandth of four-hundred-thousand. My father routinely forgot I existed. And he kept my mother from me."

"You grew resentful," the cockroach extends.

"I did. He took away my David Hasselhoff action figures. He always lorded his power over me."

"Was that why you cut his penis off and stitched it to your navel?" He pulls the strings that arch the eyebrows of his mask. His many legs wriggle.

I don't respond. I lie on the couch, one hand slid inside my shirt to hold my belly button. It's an outie.

My father says, "I have a surprise guest." He rises from his chair and twitches toward the closet. When he returns, he is holding a porcelain vase. The vase is tall and fat. Wide-mouthed. Red and black with a pattern of circles and arches and breasts.

"Mother..."

My father lays her on the table next to the couch. She stares at me, silent. The cockroach's eyes go back and forth between us.

Slowly, my belly button rises, grows stiff.

I jump up from the couch and point a finger at my father. "You bastard!" I shout, and rush at him.

The cockroach rips off its mask. My father's long, pointy beard confronts me. I pull a gun from my front pocket and shoot him. He collapses, clutching a blooming flower of blood on his thorax.

"Good," he says, gasping. "We're finally getting to the bottom of this deep-seated issue."

I shoot him again.

"Good, good," he says.

A crucifix hangs on the wall above two candlesticks. On the table sits a vase. I pick it up and lower its wide dark mouth onto my erect belly button.

The cockroach says, "You've made wonderful progress." And then it dies. It takes me twenty minutes to eat the cockroach's corpse, and another five to scrape the name off the office door and replace it with my own.

James Brown Saves Christmas

"Get up!"

"Get on up?"

"Get up!" shouts James Brown again, "it's Christmas!"

"Holy shit!" I say, and jump out of bed, throwing off the covers and rising straight up like Nosferatu. "Christmas!"

We run downstairs, James Brown in the lead. His face is all sweaty. He screams, "Stay on the scene!"

And by "the scene," he means: Christmas morning!

We each have one present under the tree. From each other. He opens his first, ripping away the paper to reveal: me!

"So good," he shouts, "so good; I got you!"

I open mine next. It's: James Brown! He doesn't wait for me to finish unwrapping him before he gets up and dances, flinging off the last bit of paper himself as he does the Mashed Potato.

Dad comes in—we haven't seen him in years—and unwraps his present (that he got for himself) to reveal: a snakeskin purse!

James Brown screams, "Papa's got a brand new bag!"

Then Dad leaves again for several more years.

We both fall silent, looking inward. I sink to the floor. The Christmas tree wilts. From the fireplace comes, not Santa Claus, but carbon monoxide.

Then James Brown does the Twist, and he looks at me and screams, "Get up!"

"Get on up?"

"Get up!" he shouts, and I do, and we both run to the kitchen and fling open the cupboards and fridge and grab flour and sugar and eggs and butter and PCP and start to make Christmas cookies!

Once the dough is ready, James Brown rolls it flat by dancing on it. Sweat drips from his face and mixes with the dough.

I feel good.

We cut shapes from the dough. We bake the shapes. We decorate the baked shapes and put them on a plate. We make hundreds of cookies of every kind. I feel nice.

James Brown picks up a gingerbread man and says, "This is a man's world!" Then he eats the gingerbread man.

We eat hundreds of cookies.

The overload of sugar and PCP turns James Brown into a monster. A vampire, to be specific. He grows fangs and dons a cape.

He attacks me. I grab a cookie shaped like a crucifix and try to ward him off. He hisses. I back him into a corner. He does the splits and wraps himself in his cape. I stand over him, holding him in place with the cookie.

A saxophonist sneaks up behind me and honks his instrument in my ear. It startles me, and while I'm distracted, James Brown bites me on the arm.

The saxophonist bows to James Brown, calls him "Master," then turns into fog and disappears into the exhaust fan over the stove.

I look at the bite on my arm. I look at James Brown.

James Brown screams, "I got you!"

Indeed; and soon I will be like him: undead!

I cry out, "My God, my God, why have you forsaken me?"

I drop to my knees. James Brown drapes a cape over me. I die.

James Brown puts me in the oven and rolls a large rock in front of it. I bake at room temperature for three days/months. Then:

"Get up..."

"Get on up?"

"Get up..." James Brown croons into my mind through vampiric telepathy; "it's Easter!"

"Holy shit!" I say, and burst out of the oven, rising from my tomb like Nosferatu. "Easter!"

We run outside and hunt for eggs and drink the blood of humans. The humans call me "Master." They are my flock. I feel good.

I knew that I would.

THE FUCKING MASTERPIECE

The board of directors negotiated with the oil magnate. Sylvia wore a black suit and said, "Mr. Baleen, we want The Fucking Masterpiece." Jonathan had a hangover and said, "We will give you the Pacific Ocean. It is worth a lot of money." Deborah was horny and said, "Sign here." Mr. Baleen signed there; he had plans for the Pacific Ocean. The board of directors drank champagne. "A toast," Jonathan said, "to The Fucking Masterpiece!" They toasted and had an orgy and ran naked through the museum, tossing jars of sulfuric acid at old works of art. Mr. Baleen had plans for the Pacific Ocean. The board of directors rented a battleship and sailed it to the Gulf of Mexico. The Fucking Masterpiece floated on the water and was visible from space. The board of directors hitched The Fucking Masterpiece to the battleship and towed it out of the Gulf of Mexico. Sondra and Charles fell overboard and drowned in the Panama Canal. Deborah had never had sex with Charles, inexplicably. The battleship reached the Pacific Ocean; it turned north. Mr. Baleen had plans for the Pacific Ocean. The board of directors put The Fucking Masterpiece on display. The Fucking Masterpiece filled the museum; it dripped from the ceiling. Visitors wore galoshes and carried umbrellas. The board of directors drank champagne. The Fucking Masterpiece dripped into their champagne glasses. They drank The Fucking Masterpiece. And Mr. Baleen had plans for the Pacific Ocean.

He drowned himself in it.

THE BAGPIPES & DRUMS OF SCOTLAND

He stopped talking to her and then spent a year still talking to her in his head. He wanted to stop talking to her in his head, so he decided he needed to talk to her.

"Hi," he said.

She said hello. She said: "How are you?"

"Insane," he answered.

They were in a virtual environment. He felt disembodied. He said, "Can we meet in person somewhere?"

"That would be awkward," she said.

"I know. Can we?"

"Where?"

They met in the parking lot of an internet café. They went in and watched a movie on the computer. There was a lot of violence. He felt like the violence was real and was happening all around and inside of him. He felt disembodied. He paused the movie to say, "Do you like the movie?"

"Yeah, I like it so far," she said. "I like all the blood and the screaming and crying and the running and falling and the begging and the laughing and the hunger and brutality and betrayal and the desolate sadness and exploitation and the mucus and feces and sweat and grease and the fear and the madness and joy," she said.

He said, "Me too."

They left after the movie and went to a park. They sat on a bench overlooking a shallow pond fringed with duck shit and cigarette butts. It was getting dark and the park lights were on.

He needed to tell her everything. He felt disembodied. He said, "When we were watching the movie I felt like we were in a virtual environment."

She said, "We were, kind of. We always are, kind of."

He nodded. He decided to tell her everything. He was going to do it. He filled his lungs, opened his mouth, and said—

—nothing, because just then a maniac sprung from the shadows and plunged a buzzing chainsaw into his face.

She came to visit him in the hospital. She said she felt terrible about the way she just sat there and screamed while the maniac sawed into his face. She said she was having nightmares about the maniac and kept seeing his big round eyes and his frozen grin and his beanie cap with the propeller on it.

"The doctors put me on meds," she laughed, "to help with the nightmares and flashbacks. But look," and she reached into the pocket of her robe, brought out a handful of pills. "I started hiding them under my tongue. Then this morning, when they let us out for fresh air, I ran."

He was motionless on a cold steel tray. He looked up at her and said nothing.

"I ran to the gift shop and bought a map of the hospital, and when I unfolded the map, it was as big as I was. And it kept redrawing itself. So it was hard to find the morgue. But I did find it. Because I had to see you."

She was all sweaty, her hospital robe dirty.

She said, "I feel disembodied."

He said nothing.

She smiled. "When I was in the ward, it felt like a virtual environment. My doctor talked about me getting out soon.

But wherever I go, it feels like that. The whole world feels like the internet."

A door banged opened somewhere near. Footfalls and voices.

She still had the pills in her hand. Each pill was a tiny maraca.

She put the entire handful in her mouth. Swallowed. The maracas rattled down her throat, into her stomach and blood.

She said, "I want to watch a movie."

She climbed on top of him on the steel tray and slid the tray back into its drawer and shut the drawer and laughed.

In the darkness, he felt her weight on him and listened to her breathing slow. He wanted to tell her everything. But his face was all ripped apart and he was dead.

Another door banged open, and voices entered the morgue. The coroner and an assistant. Music started. They liked music while they worked. Always the same music, too—an album he recognized, called *The Bagpipes & Drums of Scotland*. The first track on the album was a bagpipe rendition of "Amazing Grace." The last track was "Scotland the Brave."

The coroner fired up a chainsaw. They were doing an autopsy.

In the cold dark drawer she laid her face in the ruins of his. This was it. This was everything now. He had made himself vulnerable—opened himself to being hurt—and now they were together, in a very real place.

The bagpipes and drums and chainsaw played on.

FORGET ME NOT, FILET MIGNON

The naked man looked at his map. The map (a labyrinth of hair-thin lines traced in black mascara on a scrap of brown paper grocery bag) said he was in the Automotive Parts Department. He lifted his eyes and scanned the aisles. The shelves held nothing but dust and ash and one dented hubcap.

Blue-gray daylight fell from the vaulted ceiling. A mutant pigeon flapped through the rafters, scraping its beak across the glass of rotting skylights. It landed atop a bank of dead fluorescents. Cooing, it lifted its tail feathers to poop. Then it spontaneously combusted. The sprinkler system detected the burning pigeon and unleashed an indoor rainstorm (complete with clouds and thunder).

The naked man looked at his map. The map broke into sodden chunks that dropped through his fingers as he lifted his face into the rain. A hole in his chest leaked black slime that smelled of decaying flowers. He forgot everything for five minutes. Then he remembered.

He turned and walked away.

Two miles later he crossed into Zone C and out of the storm. He zigzagged through the lanes until he reached the Summer Fun Department, where he found an aisle whose rust-heavy shelves still held a few moldering beach towels. He dried himself, threw the towel at a spider web, and walked on through the monochrome gloom.

A clump of jungle had risen through the floor of the Pink Lingerie Department. Neon flowers hung on the steam. The naked man picked a blue forget-me-not and carried it away.

An hour's journey and he was back in Zone A. The stench of rancid meat singed his nose hair as he entered the Edible Flesh Department. He gazed into an inoperative meat cooler at scattered steaks growing gray-green afros beneath their cling wrap. He reached for a sirloin, changed his mind—he'd already done sirloin twice that week—and picked up a round steak instead.

As he was nearing the checkout, a jaguar-like growl erupted from the PA system. It ended. He passed the cart corral, where a flock of battered shopping carts was trembling as if in a private earthquake, metal cages rattling weakly.

The checkout lanes numbered in the thousands. The naked man approached one of them. Behind the counter stood a naked woman in a catatonic state.

She had one eyelash.

The man leaned toward her over the counter. He laid aside the blue forget-me-not and tore open the steak. The meat hissed as the air hit it. He shaped it into a ball.

There was a hole in the woman's head—a jagged aperture in the crown of her skull, half hidden by a thin spread of hair. Near the edge, a maggot writhed in old blood. The man flicked away the maggot. He dropped the ball of steak into the hole. He stepped back and waited.

The woman blinked.

Her mouth moved. She took a deep breath. And coughed. Couldn't stop coughing. She bent, holding her shuddering abdomen. Finally a glob of something green and red loosed itself from her lungs and flew to the floor. She sucked air. Chest movements slowing, she licked her lips and cleared her throat. Calm.

Her eyes found the naked man. For a moment she was silent. Then:

"Hello," she said. "How may I help you?"

He picked up the blue forget-me-not. "I want to buy this."

He gave her the flower. She tried to scan the barcode, but there was no barcode. "Did you peel the sticker off?" She shook the scan gun at the flower. "Where's the price tag?"

"Price tag?"

She swung her head around, peering up and down the thousands of empty checkouts. No one to help her. "I think there's a sale. I think flowers got marked down. They're free. Here." And she handed back the flower.

They stared at each other. A bee crawled out of the hole in the man's chest.

"I'd like a bag," he said. "Please."

She took the flower and put it in a brown paper grocery bag.

"Will you help me carry it to my car?"

"If you tip me. Will you tip me?"

"Handsomely."

They walked outside, flesh tightening in the chill. The air was motionless, the sky a chalk-colored dome. Asphalt stretched to the horizon, peppered lightly with dead cars, exploded shopping carts, trash bags, boulders, ribcages.

A red battle tank was parked nearby. The man pointed to it, said, "That's me."

"Does that thing work?" The woman swept at a maggot that had tumbled off her scalp and onto her shoulder. "The gun. Can you shoot stuff?"

"I'll show you. Come on."

They crossed the lot and climbed a short ladder on the side of the battle tank. The man opened a hatch on top of the gun turret. He lowered himself inside. The woman followed, closing the hatch behind her.

A light bulb (pink-tinted) flickered on inside the tank. They sat in the close space with their bare legs touching. Warmth poured from an electric fireplace behind them. The woman still had the bag with the flower in it. She took the flower out of the bag and put it in a vase with some water and put the vase on a small nightstand beside her. She looked around and said, "Cozy."

The man opened an ammunition compartment in the floor. Half a dozen human fetuses lay curled inside. He selected a fetus and loaded it into the tank's gun. "Watch," he said.

There was a window above the loveseat. The woman drew open the curtains, raised the blinds, and looked outside. The man situated himself at the gun's controls (a computer mouse and a piano keyboard). He played an F# on the piano, and the gun fired. The woman watched through the window as a fetus rocketed from the barrel and traced an arc against the gray sky.

The fetus hit the asphalt, shattering into red giblets that skipped away like rocks across a pond.

"Michael," she sighed.

"You should really stop naming them." He sat back from the controls. "Anyway, the gun works."

"You didn't need to do that. I knew it worked. I just forgot. I forget things. You know I forget things. It's your fault I forget things. Asshole."

He didn't reply. She lowered the blinds and drew the curtains and they sat in the warm pink light. He could smell the steak rotting in her brain cavity. Filth streaked her body. His too.

He said: "Will you have sex with me?"

"If you tip me. Will you tip me?"

"I will give you a very large tip."

They had sex inside the red battle tank.

His sperm fertilized seven eggs. The zygotes crackled like microscopic fireworks. Within five minutes they had grown into mango-sized fetuses. In an hour the fetuses would be the size of German Shepherd puppies.

"You need more breasts," he said. He ran a finger along the bulge of her stomach. A sweaty strand of her hair stuck to his cheek. "Like, at least four more."

"I don't even need the two I have. You know that." Her belly thundered. "Stillbirths don't need to suckle. And my milk is probably acid anyway."

She sat up in bed and grabbed her book from the nightstand (a dog-eared copy of *Great Expectations*). She found her place and started to read. He waited five pages. Then:

"You're ignoring me."

"I don't like you."

"Why?"

"Because you smashed my skull in with a golf club and ran off with my brain." She closed her book. "Then you tried to copy my brain in the key copier. Which turned it to pulp."

"I'm sorry. I was mad because you were smarter than me."

"You were mad because I tore out your heart."

"No. That happened after the brain thing. In retaliation, I think."

"I don't remember." She returned her book to the nightstand. "I feel so dull. Why don't you choose higher quality cuts of meat? I bet I could really do some deep thinking with a nice filet mignon between my ears."

Her belly expanded to the size of a pumpkin. Something kicked within, the sound like a muffled drum.

"Never mind filet mignon," he said. "We can be whole again. You can be a genius again, and I can be an emotional lunatic again. I just need to find the Human Parts Department."

"Zone XX. Behind the Ultraviolent Revenge Department. I've already told you."

"I can't find it. There's no damn logic to that place. The zones shift around at random." In his head he heard a jaguar growl. "I need you to draw a new map. The last one fell apart in the rain."

"Rain. Fire. Wind. An eagle swooping down and tearing the map from your hands. It's always something."

"Here," he said, and handed her the bag that had held the forget-me-not.

She tore the bag into scraps, surveyed the scraps, and selected the largest (it was shaped like Antarctica). She reached up and plucked her lone eyelash. Pinching the lash between thumb and forefinger, she bent over the scrap of brown paper.

A fly buzzed in her brain cavity.

"Awkward way to draw a map," he said, watching her hand move.

"A pen or pencil would be nice. But the pens are out of ink, and the pencils are broken. And someone or something stole all the crayons. My body is all that's left." She passed him her work. Trails of mascara wandered the page in an exploding snarl. She lifted her finger, the spent eyelash clinging to its tip, and said, "Make a wish."

He made a wish, and she blew the lash into the air.

"That was your last," he said.

"I know." She grimaced as her belly inflated another few inches. "Ouch."

He stared into the heart of the map. There, sunken within a vortex of paths, the Human Parts Department reared its hairy shelves. Near its perimeter, a cat-like shape stalked beneath the letters of a warning: *Here Be Dragons*.

"A brain," he said. He looked at her. "A real brain. With real neurotransmitters. Dopamine and serotonin. Remember dopamine and serotonin?"

"Empty shelves. That's what you'll find there. Oh, maybe a few appendixes or tonsils. Six-packs of wisdom teeth and pinky toes. Useless garbage. No brains, no hearts. Everything of value has disappeared, from everywhere. You know that. What makes you think the Human Parts Department will be any different?"

He didn't answer. He eyed the cat on the map.

"I want a heart," he said, quieter.

She reached toward the nightstand and plucked the blue forget-me-not from its vase. She pushed the flower through the hole in his chest, planting it in the soil between his lungs. "Satisfied?"

"I want a heart that won't decay in two days."

"I can feel two flies fucking on the piece of rotten steak I call my brain. Stop bitching."

He listened to the sounds that rolled within her head, the demonic buzzing and swampy burbles. "Have the maggots almost finished their dinner?"

"I think so. They ate all the childhood memories. Now they're gobbling up the rational faculties. Motor functions are for dessert. I'll have to go soon." Suddenly she gasped, hands clutching her enormous stomach. "Ouch. Michael just kicked me in the pancreas."

"Stop naming them," he repeated. "At least, stop naming them all Michael."

"It's my favorite name." She gasped again. "Ouch. Shit. *Shit shit shit.*"

Her vagina belched and seven Michaels fell out, strangled in their umbilical cords.

"Ouch," she said. Her belly deflated, hissing like a

punctured tire. Soon it was flat and smooth again. She stared at her dead children. "What are those?"

"Bullets."

She looked at him. "Who are you?"

"Time to go," he said.

He stood and opened the hatch. Inside the tank, the pink light flickered out. Grayness came in. He helped her climb through the hatch. She stood on the ladder leading down to the asphalt. She looked at him. Maggots squirmed in her hair.

"Had fun," she said. Drool spilled down her chin. "We will again?"

He looked into her lashless eyes. "We will. Somehow."

She smiled. "I go back to work," she said. "Job. Store." She climbed down the ladder and started across the parking lot. Her body canted to one side, off balance. She stumbled a few times. A galaxy of flies orbited her head.

He watched her until she was to the door. Then he lowered himself back into the tank. He picked up the map she had drawn. Already inaccurate, probably. There could be no map of a place with indefinite form. He knew that. The map was desperation, was fear of having to negotiate the shifting wastes unaided. The map was a lie.

He let it fall to the floor.

And he imagined:

His red battle tank screaming through the wall, empty magazine and candy racks flying as he rolled over cashier stands. He would stop briefly so that a naked woman could join him (he would have to help her aboard, carrying her inanimate body like a mannequin). Then he would make no more stops, smashing through everything as he barreled toward the heart of the place in an arrow-straight line— tunneling deep into the darker parts, into swamps and fangs and a feline cry—gun fully loaded with Michaels—no map.

He had imagined it all before.

He gathered the dead Michaels and stacked them in the ammunition compartment. Something on the floor caught his attention. He picked it up.

Against his palm, the eyelash weighed nothing. It looked like the fuse of a failed explosive.

He thought of the wish he had made. Always the same wish. Always failing to go off.

In his chest, a temporary heart thrashed on its stalk, raining petals.

He wished his wish again, then blew the eyelash into outer space. On the floor, the map spontaneously combusted. He slid behind the tank's controls and pushed a button.

The red battle tank screamed.

TO QUIT THE CHAMELEON PICNIC

Fathers always pass their wisdom on. They have to, no stopping it. It has the force of a bowel movement, and is just as pungent and embarrassing. They get an alarmed look and grunt a little and suddenly wisdom comes plopping out of their mouth, landing with a wet smack on the floor.

We both stare at it. One of us has to clean it up, and it won't be him. He's too embarrassed. He clears his throat, checks his watch, then shuffles away, mumbling something about taxes.

The wisdom is the size and shape of a small potato. It pulsates like a heart. Its body bristles with muddy fur, wiry twigs jutting from it like feelers. It creeps toward me across the kitchen tile, inching imperceptibly, a trail of slime extending behind it. It has spider eyes and a tiny toothless mouth. It smells like halitosis and plastic.

I grab a roll of paper towels. I unwind sheet after sheet, building a mitt the thickness of a book. Even through so many layers, the heat of the wisdom reaches my palm, a wet and unholy heat, and I race to the trash and dump the wisdom in and cover it with more paper towels. Then I wipe up the slime from the tile, which takes a long time because the slime has already congealed and clings to the floor like tissue to bone.

Dad comes back, sees me still cleaning up his mess,

and says, "The taxes," then starts to turn and leave again. But another bolus of wisdom escapes his mouth along with the words, emerging like a surprise burp. I am on the floor, wiping up slime, my father above me as the wisdom drops from him. No time to dodge it. It lands on my head.

I scream, disgusted with existence, with my particular existence. The wet lump glues itself to my head. It throbs, hot. I tear at it, and it bites my hand. Its wiry feelers pierce down into my skull, into my brain.

My father shouts, "The taxes!" And he turns to flee.

I jump at his legs, knocking him down before he can escape. I climb over him and push my face into his, shouting, "We have to talk!" My brain fills with wires, with common words. "Help me!"

He sighs, closes his eyes.

His head starts to inflate.

I back away from the ballooning head, but it keeps coming, expanding toward me as I scramble backward across the kitchen floor. As the eyes grow huge, I can see into them. There is a picnic happening down among the rods and cones, an eternal picnic imprinted on the red, green, and blue flowers, my father and my mother on a blanket sharing fruit and meat and talking for long hours. My father must see this always, the way spots sometimes form in our vision and never leave.

His retinas wilt, the rods and cones drooping, and the tiny picnic ends, two corpses decomposing and a wind lifting the blanket away to nowhere, scraps blowing like crows through the concave sky.

His head almost fills the kitchen now. A nostril tries to engulf my foot, and I kick it. I hate this, hate seeing this. I have seen heads inflate before, several throughout my life. My kindergarten teacher, Mrs. Hegel—it happened to her, in front of all the kids. It's what happens when a person gives up, truly gives up. It's embarrassing to see.

"Dad, stop!"

He doesn't, of course. He's given up.

I squeeze past his enormous head, pushing with my elbows and fists, and make it out of the kitchen. I know what happens next—what happened to Mrs. Hegel—and I don't wait around for it, my focus moving on, my mind on myself as I hurry from the house to the garage. There came a point, just as her head was crushing us to death against the walls of the classroom, when the substance of Mrs. Hegel changed, her ballooning head breaking apart into a mass of chameleons. The chameleons scattered throughout the room, taking on the colors of their surroundings, dispersing into invisibility, an irrevocable blending of lizard and world. There were flowers on the sill, red, green, and blue, and a lizard stopped in front of them, shrouded itself in their appearance, and never moved again. That was the way it happened. The way it always happens. The pieces of a head crawl apart and hide.

In the garage, I dump a toolbox on the ground and sift through the confusion until I find a broken wine bottle. For all the wisdom he coughed up involuntarily, my father never taught me about tools. But this broken wine bottle looks right, something about it inherently suited to my purpose. There is even some scent remaining, and in a second I can name it: cabernet sauvignon. It was my mother's favorite.

I use the broken bottle as a knife to hack at the wisdom attached to my head. The wisdom squirts blood, crying through its tiny toothless mouth. Its blood is full of explosions and boredom. My scalp bleeds also, because I am not being very careful, but there is nothing in my blood, neither explosions nor boredom, picnics nor lizards. I slice at the wisdom until it stops crying, and then I reach up and grasp its dead little body, and I pull.

The garage fills with exhaust.

The dead little body rips loose from my head. I toss it away and inspect my bloody scalp. The wires are still in my skull, broken off inside, their exposed ends too short and slippery to grip. Dead, the wires reach deep into my brain, deeper than I can feel.

The exhaust makes me cough. There's no ventilation in here. Also, no car. We got rid of the car. We had to, after Mom. Straight to the junkyard it went, its upholstery still reeking of the fumes of oblivion. Straight to scrap, because it made us sick to think of anyone driving it ever again.

Coughing, I go to open a window. But every time I reach for it, the window leaps away. The door, too, leaps away when I try to apprehend it. No way out; no way to get air. I have to at least shut the car off, then.

But we got rid of the car.

My vision doubles, then quadruples, then starts to crackle with black pinholes. I slump to the floor. So tired, going under the waves. It would feel nice to sleep... to just give up and sleep... to quit all this...

No!

I jump up and stumble around and run into something large and solid in the middle of the garage. Something invisible. My hands inspect the invisible thing, following its contours and learning its textures, and in a second I can name it: a car. A car made of chameleons.

I find the door and climb in, then search blindly for the ignition. My hand closes on the key, and I turn it toward me to kill the engine, to stop the fumes and the fog forever. But the key is already turned off. The engine is not actually running.

The wires in my brain, the exhaust in the garage—

somehow the two are interrelated. Different densities of one substance. My father and my mother. Line and plane. Order, chaos, sun, moon. No, I don't know.

My head starts to inflate.

"Stop! Stop! Stop!"

I keep trying to kill the engine, but of course the engine is already dead. So I turn the key the other way, and the engine starts, sounding like trumpets and kettledrums. Slowly, the air begins to clear. The exhaust returns to its source, sucked by invisible tailpipes back into the invisible car.

But my head—it doesn't stop. It overtakes space, installing itself in the emptiness. It fills the car. The car made of chameleons. A lizard (the rearview mirror) flashes briefly into visibility, a red shimmer passing through it, then a green, then a blue. Down among the meadows of my retinas, I am having a picnic by myself.

Why? How did this happen? I never made the conscious decision to give up. To quit space and time and animality. No, something made the decision for me, without my consent or awareness. As if my shadow signed a contract binding to the whole. No, I don't know.

I blame my father.

Do not give up. Fight it. Fight the neutralization, the homogenization of space. Dive into the energy of external phenomena. Find things to do.

I turn on the radio. I sing along. I change the station. I contemplate an advertisement. I slam my fists into the steering wheel. I run the windshield wipers (two long chameleon tails) for no reason. I clean gunk from the cup holders. I organize the glove compartment.

I go for a drive.

The car crashes through the garage wall and into the house, coming to a stop in the living room. There it breaks apart, its reptilian pieces dispersing to become the room, to freeze into the couch and the clock and the television.

In the kitchen, my father is a mass of chameleons, hidden.

Stacks of paper rain from the ceiling. The taxes.

I do the taxes.

My head fills the room, flowing over the couch and the clock and the television. I dive into the energy of the taxes, vomiting scrawls of ink at random. This is embarrassing. I hate this, hate being this. This is all that my wisdom amounts to. I do the taxes. Disgust. I do the taxes. Camouflage.

I do the taxes.

And then I quit.

art and science

Maggie became a terrorist in the fifth grade. That was the year she read the Manifesto. When she was supposed to be doing her homework, when she was supposed to be drawing hearts around the name of her crush (Mr. Kool, the math teacher), she was instead reading the Manifesto.

Mrs. Winston (social studies) said, "Maggie, come to the front of the class and do something smart."

"I'm reading the Manifesto, you fascist!"

Mrs. Winston hit Maggie with a nightstick, knocking out most of her hundreds of teeth. Maggie swallowed the teeth before anyone could claim them. She didn't want her teeth used for science (Mr. Salem) or art (Mrs. Marlboro).

The missing teeth made lunch difficult. She could not eat the diced boots or the shredded belts. She tried the heel of a boiled sock, could only suck its juices toothlessly. The bell rang to end lunch, and Maggie faced a long afternoon on low fuel.

She fell asleep in phys ed (Mr. Camel). Jerking awake, she glanced around in worry, but no one had noted her dozing, even though they were in the middle of dodgeball and she had passed out center court. She found shoe imprints all over her. New bruises.

Also new: a sutured incision running from sternum to pubis.

In science, they dissected teeth. Maggie thought she recognized a stain on one of the teeth. She took the tooth to

Mr. Salem and said, "Is this my incisor, you fascist?"

Mr. Salem hit her with a nightstick. He assigned her extra homework.

In art, they made decorative masks—out of teeth. Maggie recognized every tooth.

She threw a handful of teeth at Mrs. Marlboro. "How did you get my teeth, you fascist? I hid them in my stomach, so how?"

"You fell asleep, you fool! Never fall asleep!"

The other children put on their decorative masks made of teeth. Dumb faces looked out through mouths and eyeholes. Maggie refused to complete her mask and received a failing grade on the project.

The last class of the day was English (Mr. Basic). They discussed word choice. Maggie ignored class and read the Manifesto, every word of which she thought chosen perfectly.

She fell asleep again, jerked awake again. Again, no one seemed to notice. But there was fresh pain in her abdominal incision, as if she had been opened and closed anew, and the other children all had on new hats made of intestines.

She turned to her favorite passage in the Manifesto, but it failed to give her strength, and her gathering tears blurred the words. She wanted a hat too.

At home that evening, her father refused to be her father, disappointed in her for all that she had lost at school.

everyday struggle

The crazy legless veteran raises an American flag every morning. As he salutes the flag, an alcoholic politician emerges from the house across the street, carrying a Cannibal Corpse t-shirt. The politician raises the t-shirt up a flagpole. The two flagpoles reach for each other, and the American flag and the t-shirt slap together in hateful struggle.

It is Christmas, and the crazy legless veteran goes caroling. He knocks on my door. "Sing me a song," he says. I say, "That's not how caroling works." He says, "I died for your sins," and he extends his arms as if crucified, each hand palming a Nine Inch Nails CD. I say, "Don't you mean you fought for my freedom?" He was in last year's war. "Also," I say, "the crucifixion is more of an Easter thing, I think." Then I sing him a Public Enemy song and he goes away.

Every morning, I watch the American flag and the Cannibal Corpse t-shirt fight, and I wonder which side I'm on. Then a bugle sounds, and I take up my butter knife.

HOW I MET YOUR DEFORMED MOTHER

You do not ring my doorbell so I have to walk outside and ring it for you and walk back inside and open the door and pretend to be surprised to see you.

"How did you get here?" I ask even though I know you took a taxi since I drove the taxi myself as I stared at you in the rearview mirror the whole time, not noticing the myriad dogs and cats and fire hydrants that passed violently beneath my front bumper

You do not look at me. Your body language oozes disinterest as you compose a text message on your cell phone. You look like someone waiting in line for fast food and/or a funeral viewing. It is going to be a very long wait. You do not look at me, even when I address you with unnecessary volume:

"Please, come in. I was just sitting down to dinner. You can join me. It will be pleasant and memorable, unforgettable, eternal. There's green bean casserole. The knives are sharp and the night is young and so are we (well, maybe not me). And this one very happy evening could determine the course of all future evenings. It could completely transform my ugly drooping world, although it almost certainly will not."

You do not come in, so I have to tow my house five

feet until you are standing in my front hallway even though you never moved. Your head continues dripping into the text messages you compose which, I notice, all consist of the words *yeah*, *okay*, *right*, and *cool*.

I grab a corner of the rug underneath you and drag the rug with you on it into the dining room.

I lied about there being green bean casserole. The only thing on the table is a bowl of sugar. Oh, and a pile of dead flies. I light two candles and set them on the table next to the flies, which are not actually dead but only wingless and legless and buzzing helplessly.

"Please," I say, indicating a wobbly chair, "have a seat."

You blow hair out of your eyes and lick your upper left molar. "I wish I had some gum," you mumble to yourself, looking at a dark stain on the ceiling, "spearmint gum."

"Imagine that!" I laugh nervously. "That just happens to be what we're having for dessert! This really is meant to be, don't you think?"

The stain on the ceiling is cat-shaped.

You do not sit, so I have to push a chair into the back of your knees so that you collapse into it with a small unconscious grunt. Then I rush around to the opposite side of the table and seat myself on a rocking horse and interlace my fingers to make a hammock on which I rest my head and smile at you.

Hours pass.

"So," I say, "what have you been up to lately?"

More hours pass.

"Fascinating," I say.

The moon goes through a full cycle of waxing and waning. You never seem to get tired of staring into your cell phone and texting all the people on your hit list. Each text is a tiny message in a bottle, an empty-headed *yeah* floating out into the ether.

Your phone battery dies, but you keep tapping the keypad and checking your inbox and playing two to three minute rounds of a knockoff version of Tetris. The black screen does not light up your face, which is probably a good thing because you are growing older every minute and there are hundreds of tiny demonic mites living in your eyebrows.

"Now for dessert," I say, and I leap across the table with a rag soaked in chloroform and close the rag over your mouth and nose until you are unconscious. Then I leave the house and sprint up the sloping street to the nearest gas station, where I purchase a pack of spearmint gum because I was lying earlier when I acted like I already had spearmint gum planned for dessert. Really, I have not owned a pack of spearmint in years. I was only trying to impress you with the extreme degree to which our tastes coincide. Luckily, you will never know it was a lie. You will never glimpse my behind-the-scenes engineering ... because you are fast asleep and dreaming.

The cashier at the gas station is wearing a shirt with a picture of a big red button on it. The words *self destruct* are written on the button. "My cat was kidnapped," he tells me as I pay for my gum. "Do you know anything about it?"

I reach across the counter and press the button on his shirt. He doesn't even have time to assume a look of horror before he is gone, seamlessly and efficiently vanished, as if the cameras stopped on a film shoot and he walked off set and the cameras started again. I wonder if he is somewhere backstage smoking a cigarette as he reflects on his performance, wishing he'd improvised more, been more expressive with his hands and face, and read some lines with more passion and others with less.

I steal a book of matches before I leave.

Returning home, it is easier to go down the street than up it because I let gravity do all the work, sucking me down the slope like I am a barrel full of pork chops. My knees and elbows and forehead scrape away on the pavement. A bone sticks out of my forearm, resembling a thick pencil that someone has snapped in half. Then the stolen book of matches in my pocket ignites and sets my clothes on fire.

I roll to a stop at the bottom of the street. I stand and brush a pebble off my shirtsleeve, trying to compose myself before going back inside to meet your sleeping form.

I go inside.

Inside, I am in the wrong house. A family of five looks up from dinner as I enter their foyer and bleed on their carpet. Above me, a smoke detector squawks, probably due to my clothes being on fire. A sprinkler system turns on, flooding the house with over a foot of water in an instant.

But it is not the right type of water to extinguish my suit of flames. Instead, it is foamy and full of goldfish and is actually orange-flavored soda.

"My apologies," I say, bowing politely and backing slowly through the door as fire engines roar to a halt and men in black and yellow armor get out to attack the house with axes.

Someone squirts me with a high-powered hose and I am no longer on fire. Now I am dripping wet and cold. My skin has gone from doughy flesh to crispy cinders. Sections of cooked meat slough off and fall to the ground like very old shingles oozing off a roof.

"I hope you all fucking burn!" I scream, running backward into the night. "I hope your flesh melts and runs like wax from the bone!"

But I forgot: the house is not actually on fire and this is just a false alarm that I caused. No one is going to burn, not the family of five or the firefighters or the dog or the cat or the spiders in the attic.

I scream, "I hope you all fucking drown then! I hope

your lungs fill with orange-flavored soda and you do not spontaneously evolve gills in order to survive!" I scream until my voice cracks. "Will all of you please just die!" But I don't stick around to see that they do, so I obviously don't care that much after all.

I spend the next three hours running through the neighborhood, trying to remember where I live. This occurs in fast forward, so it really only takes maybe three or four minutes.

A homeless man stops me and offers to sell me a map to my house. We do business. On the map, there is a star with the words *you are here, you are home!* written inside it.

Lowering the map, I look up. My house is right in front of me. I thank the homeless man and fold the map into a paper airplane and sail the airplane toward the homeless man. He catches it with his eye, which pops and gushes some substance resembling egg whites.

I hurry inside.

You are no longer unconscious. You have crawled onto the table and assumed the posture of a roasted pig with an apple in its mouth. But instead of an apple, you have your cell phone. The screen faces outward between your stretched and splitting lips. The screen glows again, as if the dead battery is recharging itself with your bioelectrical energy.

We are silent, staring at each other.

"How are you?" I ask even though it does not feel like the right thing to say and saying it makes the plates of my skull feel as if they do not fit together properly. "How are things?"

You do not reply by speaking. Instead, a text message forms itself on the screen of your phone. I lean in closer to read it:

where's dessert?

"Oh," I say, and reach into a charred pocket for the package of spearmint gum. But the gum is not there. It melted in my fire. It is gone. Goner than gone.

I have ruined our future.

I collapse to the floor, weeping.

"I'm sorry," I say through the snot and tears. "I just wanted to make you happy." It is difficult to breathe. "I am such an idiot fucking failure chump." My fingers rake at my skull.

You say, *i hate you.*

I nod. I know, I know.

You say, *you're a creep.*

I nod. I nod enthusiastically. Yes, yes.

do you like me?

"I adore you," I say.

you never told me.

"You would have   rejected me."

yes i would have.

"I am going to kill myself now."

this was a nice dinner.

"What?" I say. "What?"

i had fun.

"You were unconscious."

i think i love you.

"That's good," I say. "It's good to love someone."

i love you so much.

"You are smothering me."

i will mutilate myself for you.

"You are becoming obsessive and sad."

you cannot escape me.

"I do not want to."

stop trying to manipulate me.

"I do not want to."

please leave me alone.

"I never will."

good. good.

"You are painfully dear to me for no apparent reason."
i hate you.
"I fucking despise you."

You accidentally swallow your phone. After that, it is impossible to communicate. We pass the night in knowing silence. It bothers me. You don't seem bothered though. You probably don't care about me.

I lie down on the floor. I roll around. The rag soaked in chloroform that I used on you is lying on the floor next to me. I accidentally roll my face in it and lose consciousness.

When I wake up two days later you are dead. You have removed your soul from your human body and put it into the bowl of sugar next to the flies. I do not like the bowl of sugar as much as I liked your human body. You were attractive.

THE SUICIDAL MOOSE

"...and this," said the pirate, introducing the moose on his shoulder, "be James."

"Hi, James," we all said in unison.

The pirate—Captain Whiskeycola—scanned the room with a bulging eye while he tapped the handle of a sword at his belt. As if daring us to ask why he had a moose on his shoulder instead of a parrot.

Someone did ask, and Captain Whiskeycola roared out of his seat and decapitated the inquirer. Even with the enormous moose on his shoulder, the pirate moved lithely. The severed head flew across the circle of chairs and landed in Susan's lap.

Captain Whiskeycola returned to his seat. He snarled at us, showing off his missing teeth and gangrenous tongue.

"Captain," said Susan, "I realize you are new to our group, but *this*"—lifting the head—"goes against our bylaws." She pointed to the EXIT sign. "Please leave."

"But I need help!" He leaked a rheumy tear into his beard. "I be an alcoholic!"

"We are all alcoholics here." She indicated the severed head. "*Scott* was an alcoholic, *he* needed help—but not *this* kind of help!"

Captain Whiskeycola roared out of his seat and decapitated Susan.

The group applauded. We all hated Susan.

Captain Whiskeycola wiped blood from his sword. He returned to his seat.

The meeting proceeded. The pirate was attentive; he genuinely wanted to be here, wanted help. But he kept a hand on his sword, just so we wouldn't forget he was a pirate.

At one point he unwrapped a Slim Jim and fed it to his moose. From where I sat, I could smell the spiced meat. And suddenly all I wanted was a drink. A familiar pain ripped at my guts and heart. It was as if all the healing I had done was a lie; that ramrod of pain in my center was the truth of my life.

I couldn't blame Captain Whiskeycola; he didn't know that Slim Jims were one of my triggers. I used to eat them all the time when I was drinking. I drank, ate Slim Jims, and watched the same two movies again and again.

That is who I am, inside.

I attend another meeting that evening: a support group for suicidal people. There are supposed to be cupcakes tonight, in honor of Bill, who is celebrating five years of not killing himself. Usually I would be excited about cupcakes, but tonight I feel no love for anything.

The group meets in the morgue of an abandoned hospital. Someone has wheeled out an old autopsy table to put the cupcakes on. Stray sprinkles dot the table like pastel maggots, and I stare at these for awhile. For some reason, the brown sprinkles make me feel the worst.

The group has a newcomer tonight: an enormous moose with a pirate on its shoulder. The pirate chugs rum from a leather bag. He doesn't recognize me from the AA meeting.

Bill asks the moose to introduce itself.

"This be James," says Captain Whiskeycola, "and he be suicidal."

"Hi, James," we all say in unison.

As the meeting proceeds, James and I are the only ones who refrain from having a cupcake.

The moose and the pirate are at my Sex Addicts meeting on Tuesday.

I never get to have real sex, but I am addicted to masturbating and watching pornography and thinking sexual thoughts about every person I see. Most who attend the Sex Addicts meeting are addicted to real sex, which I don't understand. To me, that's like being addicted to heroin when all the heroin in the world is locked up in impregnable safes. Honestly, I should probably not be here: listening to these people talk about real sex does nothing but deepen my obsession.

Tonight, the moose and the pirate somehow perch on each other simultaneously, their bodies knotted in a deranged display of contortionism. Looking at them, my mind feels squirmy, shuddery, like there are stiff jellied trout flopping up my brainstem.

Throughout the meeting, James and Captain Whiskeycola do nothing but stare at me.

Later, I cut through alleys on my way home. Night has fully bloomed. The alleyways are dim with secondhand light. Ancient garbage swells from every corner like prolific fungus, and sinewy cats launch from shadow to shadow.

My route home is labyrinthine. I get lost. I try to orient myself by the sound of roaring flames from a building always on fire near mine. The burning building has guided me home many times before, but tonight something is wrong. I keep losing track of the sound.

Ahead, something steps out from behind a mountain of trash.

It is James and Captain Whiskeycola, still knotted

together in that impossible loop, each perched on the other. They approach me, lumbering forward on haphazard arms and legs. The pirate chugs rum from a rusty flask, his eyes bleary, and the moose bleeds from open wrists. From somewhere out of that flux of bodies, an enraged penis juts, and I cannot tell if it belongs to moose, man, or both.

I know I should run, but I feel immobilized. Caged by inertia. This feeling, it reminds me of all the nights I sat alone in my room, in just my boxer shorts, getting drunk while watching *The Driller Killer* for the thousandth time, passing out and drooling on myself. It is a feeling of zero momentum—of being paralyzed in space-time as my life bleeds out. No support group can cure me of this feeling.

It is who I am, inside.

The moose-pirate tackles me to the ground. My face lands in garbage. An enormous weight climbs on top of me, and my clothes fall away before an eager flurry of hands, blades, and antlers. Hooves pin me down. I have no volition.

The moose-pirate rapes me for an hour or so. I fade in and out. I think I am violated with a Slim Jim at one point. This feels like the end of my life.

Another fade-out, another fade-in, and the moose-pirate is gone. Must have finished while my mind was away. For awhile I just lie there in the garbage, feeling like a part of it. Eventually I drag myself up, gather the tatters of my clothes, and stumble home. I follow the sound of the burning building.

Captain Whiskeycola and his moose are not present at my next AA meeting. Everyone worries that Captain Whiskeycola has fallen off the wagon. The pirate is pretty popular here for killing Susan. Does anyone have his number? Maybe we should call him. We have to take care of our own. Has anyone seen him?

The entire meeting centers on the whereabouts of Captain Whiskeycola, so I never get to discuss the slip I had. The night after the incident in the alleyway, I stayed in and drank multiple bottles of wine while watching *Don't Go in the House*. All week I've been dreading confession, but it seems my dread was a waste. There is no room for me on the agenda.

Later that evening, James and his pirate are absent from the meeting of suicidal people. Everyone fears the worst. Bill assigns some of us to watch the obituaries.

When Tuesday rolls around again, I decide not to go to my Sex Addicts meeting. I stay home and listen to the inferno next door. I take some sleeping pills.

THE SUICIDAL CAT

Erwin blinked. Ten seconds later, he blinked again. The wall was two inches from his nose, close enough to brush with his whiskers, but he could barely see it through the murk. Not that he wanted to see it, or needed to, having long since memorized its every stretch of psoriatic plaster. He occupied his mind by blinking in precise intervals.

Behind him, the door opened. He shuttered his eyes against the sudden light. Sticky simian hands encircled his torso and lifted him from the floor.

"How's, my, little, kitty?" a tuneless falsetto inquired. "Yes-yes, la-la, *kiss-kiss-kiss*," this last accompanied by actual kisses. He creased his brow, feeling the waxy deposits of lipstick sully his fur.

She bent to inspect his food bowl.

"Erwin, baby," she cooed, framing his face in her hands. "Why aren't you eating? Are you sick?" She ran a hand across his forehead as if to check for fever.

He blinked.

The man appeared behind the woman, his caterpillar mustache closed upon a pipe stem. "Still not eating, hmm?" He flashed a cheesy grin. "Well, let's take him to the vet." The grin fell. "This could get pricey." He scratched his chin in contemplation. "He might need an operation."

Erwin blinked.

"A special diet," the man said, mustache wriggling on top of his pipe. "Medicine three times daily."

Erwin winced as the woman *kiss-kiss-kissed* him.

The man removed his pipe. "Euthanasia," he intoned.

"Well," said the woman, "whatever it takes. Nothing is too much for our"—*kiss*—"little"—*kiss*—"Mister"—*kiss*—"Kitty."

Erwin thought, *No, no, no.*

He kicked loose of the woman's hold, ran to his food bowl in the corner of the closet, and started to chow down, peering sidewise to make sure they saw him.

"Hmm." Pipe back in mouth. "Miraculous recovery."

The closet door creaked shut.

After several weeks of faking a healthy appetite, Erwin actually developed one. After several more weeks, his appetite was unhealthy again, but on the opposite end of the spectrum. He ate ceaselessly. The woman, mistaking this as a positive turn and wishing to nurture it, supplied an endless flow of Meow Mix.

One day, Erwin no longer fit into his old jeans.

The house was five thousand square feet. Erwin typically occupied only one or two of those squares. Occasionally he sojourned to the small rug in front of the refrigerator to listen to the compressor hum.

He stared at the rug's floral pattern. A month ago, his belly had ended at the tulips; now, it extended well into the roses, a mudslide of calico eclipsing the red bouquet.

He wanted ice cream.

Behind him, the kitchen table creaked rhythmically. He rolled his head to look. The woman lay naked on the table, moaning a tuneless falsetto as the man, pipe in mouth, thrust his barbed penis between her legs. Her nipples dribbled watery milk.

Erwin blinked. Without his consent, that libidinous

tendon flexed that connected his head, heart, and loins.

He retreated to his closet and shut the door. The kitchen was just down the hall, the man and woman still audible. Erwin stroked his penis, pressing his ear against the door to gather in the sound of slapping flesh and labored breathing.

He looked down, wanting to see his penis in his hand, but his belly obstructed the view. His arm grew tired. His penis grew soft. He stopped masturbating.

In the kitchen, the woman said, "Yes-yes!"

The man said, "Indeed!"

Erwin was a virgin.

He crawled into the corner where his thin mattress waited. He put on headphones and listened to "Vesti la giubba" from *Pagliacci*.

The boy and his friends liked to smoke catnip in the basement. Erwin supplied the catnip to them in exchange for whiskey. The boy, a handsome football player, had started hinting to Erwin that he was looking to score some Rohypnol. Erwin hinted back that he was looking for a gun.

The girl liked to chase a ball of yarn around her room. One day the yarn disappeared. The girl cried for hours, stopping only when the yarn suddenly reappeared after Erwin failed for the hundredth time to tie a noose with it.

Erwin smelled gas.

He blinked. He had been sleeping, sort of. His groin throbbed with the fading dream of a Siamese in estrus. His head throbbed with last night's whiskey. The smell of gas made him think of deathless machinery.

He tracked the smell to the kitchen.

The oven door stood open, four bodies kneeling with

their heads stuffed into the gas-filled darkness. On the table was a note, the penmanship exquisite:

Midway through our evening game of Monopoly, *we separately and simultaneously came to a full realization of the futility of existence. With this in view, we have decided to take the most logical action. In my left rear pocket you will find a check for $20,000 and a full account of debts owed. Thank you.*

Erwin turned off the gas and opened a window. He sat and stared at the four dead buttocks slumped before the oven. He licked a paw, ran the wetted limb through his fur.

He pulled the woman's pants down.

Erwin had requested only one bullet for the gun, but the boy had produced an entire case, claiming, "They don't sell single bullets at Wal-Mart." He had thanked Erwin for the Rohypnol and left for his date.

Erwin contemplated the gun now. He took one bullet and loaded it into the chamber. He contemplated the gun.

He contemplated.

To help him contemplate, he put on Pachelbel's *Canon.* The strings built slowly over the ground bass as Erwin reviewed his life.

Outside, a siren wailed. Boots stomped. Erwin looked through the open window and saw a phalanx of Nazis marching up the street. He thought of deathless machinery.

A fanged Nazi appeared at the window, waving his rifle and screaming in German.

Erwin looked at the bullets on the table. He had wanted but one, gotten a case of infinite. And he hated Nazis almost as much as he hated himself.

He contemplated.

He raised his gun. He blinked.

A shot rang out.

GRAND THEFT AUTO: VICE CITY

All Tony Warlord wants is to run the game. He cracks a beer and listens for his Pizza Rolls to ding, done. Shades drawn. On TV a woman dies, his doing. The controller shakes to simulate a neck atremble. His palms have dulled the lustrous plastic, shiny black to matte, just as knees or lips will burnish a point of prayer or tribute. He steals a car, crushes a kid against a brick wall—the controller shakes. He kills a cop then fucks and kills a prostitute (stealing his money back) and steers a car at her corpse to kill her more; but the corpse disappears before he can crunch over it. That's fucked up; the game designers oughta change that. What good is making someone dead if you can't have their body to play with forever? The bodies should linger and rot for all time, till bones choke the memory chips. Fuck, unfair.

Ding.

Tony Warlord struggles up from his armchair. He comes back with Pizza Rolls and burns the roof of his mouth on them. His tongue, too. He shoots someone who owes someone money. He steals a car, goes to the nightclub, disappears into the bathroom (it's implied he's doing coke, probably) for several seconds, shoots ten to twenty people in the nightclub before the cops show up, shoots the cops, dies, respawns, jumps up from his armchair, shouts, "I am the Lord and I've done things that most men only dream about!" Then he falls back into his chair and into a nap.

He forgets to press pause.

A knock on the door stirs him. He answers it.

And stands facing himself.

In the hall outside his apartment, there he is: Tony Warlord.

Tony Warlord (the one outside) says to Tony Warlord (the one inside): "You're boring. The game designers thought they oughta change you." He raises a gun and shoots Tony Warlord in his neural circuitry.

Ding.

Tony Warlord steps inside, over the corpse of Tony Warlord, and shuts the door. The corpse disappears before Tony Warlord can kill it more. "Fucking shame," he mutters, addressing his vanished self, "that I can't strip you and scissor your dead dick off."

Looking for something to do, Tony Warlord explores his apartment. His dominion. He steals the armchair, pulling a little old lady out of it and beating her to death with a toilet plunger, then cruises around the living room, channel surfing on the radio (80s music, mostly, cuz this is a period piece) and swerving into end tables, before crashing the armchair into the kitchen wall. He bails. A cop's been on his tail for two minutes, from when he hit a pedestrian by the TV, and the pig catches up with him now. Tony Warlord escapes into the refrigerator. He completes a mission wherein he eats three slices of the deli ham folded over with a squirt of mustard in the center; then, for fun, he cuts two segments of cheddar from the block and eats them plain—inadvertently uncovering a whole world of side missions hidden in the block of cheese... molecular side missions for his physiology to metabolize while his psychology advances the main narrative...

A knock on the refrigerator door. He answers it.

And stands facing himself.

In the kitchen outside the refrigerator, there he is: Tony Warlord.

"You're repeating the same mistakes," says the Tony Warlord outside to the Tony Warlord inside. "I'm our last chance. Our last life." He raises a gun and shoots out the refrigerator light, and all the food goes instantly bad, including the deli ham and the cheddar and the Tony Warlord inside. All the bad food, including him, disappears, cleared off the map. Flushed from the memory chips. Damn shame that it can't all be kept, all the beautiful bones of things.

Tony Warlord faces the empty refrigerator and says, "I am the Lord and I'm hungry." He tips the toaster upside down and eats the rain of burnt crumbs (and it's implied he gets high from them) and fucks and kills the toaster and steers a vacuum cleaner at a kid, his kid, to crush his kid against the brick wall that is the TV screen. His kid's corpse disappears, and Tony Warlord vacuums the spot where it was. His knuckles bulge whitely on the handle of the vacuum cleaner as he grips it like it's a crucifix versus a vampire. His palms have dulled the lustrous plastic. He goes to the nightclub in the cupboard and shoots ten to twenty people, all him. He fucks a prostitute in the overflowing trash and steals a car in the middle of traffic (the traffic that runs in the cracks, in the seams where grease and hair and spiders collect). He engages in vice on multiple levels because to not do so is to lose agency as a character. He equates his horizons with those of his apartment, which is his city.

He runs his city—until the dirty laundry stages a coup against him.

He cameos in the sequel as a minor character who drinks beer and eats Pizza Rolls and bemoans the loss of a glory he never had. When he dies, his body leaves the map after a two-second wake.

No respawn.

Self-contained Underwater Breathing Apparatus

Contempt is a natural enough response to anything, but it is an especially natural response to a scuba diver who is having sex with your wife—especially if your wife is in a coma, and especially if the scuba diver has webbed feet.

"You!" I shout. "Scuba diver! Cease this rape!"

He doesn't listen, pretending he has water in his ears. Or maybe he really does have water in his ears. He is a scuba diver, after all. He is clearly out of his element, flopping like a fish on top of my wife in her hospital bed.

I swing out at his flailing limbs and grasp a webbed foot. The foot comes off and I realize that it is not really a foot but a plastic swimfin. How silly of me, to think that a human being would have an elongated foot with bright yellow webbing between the toes.

But then I see the foot that was inside the swimfin, and indeed it is elongated with bright yellow webbing between the toes.

Perhaps I am wiser than I know.

I swing out again, grasp the foot again. It comes off, and I realize that it is not really a foot but yet another plastic swimfin that the scuba diver was wearing underneath the first swimfin. Silly me—duped two times in as many seconds. I honestly believed that this human being's foot was elongated with bright yellow webbing between the toes...

But then I see the foot that was inside the swimfin that was inside the first swimfin, and indeed it is elongated with bright yellow webbing between the toes.

I swing out, grab the foot. It comes off—a swimfin—and the foot underneath it is, once again, elongated with bright yellow webbing between the toes. I drop the swimfin, swing out, grab the foot. The foot comes off—a fourth swimfin.

The scuba diver's wetsuit is wet and goes *squish-squish* as the scuba diver flops like a fish on top of my wife in her hospital bed. I pull swimfin after swimfin from the end of the scuba diver's flailing leg. The floor is quickly filling up with the bright yellow appendages, and I am starting to doubt that I will ever reach a true foot, if there is such a thing as a true foot...

Frustrated, I throw down the one hundred and eleventh swimfin and, crossing my arms over my chest, shout, "No more!" This elicits no response from the scuba diver, who continues to rape my wife. He is a poor rapist. His technique is all wrong. I shout at him: "Where did you learn to rape, anyhow!"

The oxygen tanks strapped to his back begin to leak, and sniffing the air I realize that they are not really tanks full of oxygen like I thought, but tanks full of farts. All of my assumptions are turning out to be wrong today.

"Why are you breathing farts?" I shout at the scuba diver, but he doesn't respond, too busy raping my wife and sucking down farts. I would call him an asshole, but he might take it as a compliment, and I certainly don't want to compliment him: I never compliment a person who has not complimented me first, and the scuba diver has certainly not complimented me—unless he considers it a compliment to rape my comatose wife.

"Excuse me!" I shout at him. "Are you trying to

compliment me?"

His goggles are full of soil and worms. His penis is not outside his wetsuit, and my wife's hospital gown is not pulled up around her waist, but he is flopping on top of her like a fish and how else can I construe this but as rape?

If my wife were conscious right now, would she enjoy this rape? Everything I know about her suggests that she might. She once had sex with a syphilitic professor of physics while I napped in the next room and dreamt of black holes. Her promiscuity was one of the reasons I had her put in a coma in the first place.

The scuba diver flops, *squish-squish* on top of my wife.

Maybe I should just leave these two alone...

No. This is an outrage, and I will no longer tolerate outrages—I've lived with them for far too long, averaging an outrage a day for the past ten years, at least. Any more outrages and I am likely to vomit all over myself (and others) like I do when I drink too many energy drinks or watch too much television.

I tap the scuba diver on the shoulder. "Sir!" Tap-tap. "Scuba diver!" Tap-tap-tap. "I insist that you cease this rape!"

Tap.

The air tanks on his undulating back are still leaking farts, filling the room with their fragrance: the aroma of fermented bowel movements, the scent of exploded septic tanks, the perfume of multitudinous pig farms.

Really, there are no words to describe the simple hell of biology.

I beat the scuba diver over the head with an IV pole, then with a metal crutch, then with a bedpan. But he is impervious to my attacks, superhuman in his slippery wetsuit, unshakable in his single-minded drive to flop on comatose women.

I might have to kill him.

But that would be irrational, and I am not irrational. Murder is the easiest way to deal with any situation, but it requires a suspension of sanity that I am just not capable of...

My sanity is tyrannical. It keeps me forever in the dungeon of intelligence. Nausea ensues with even the smallest indiscretion—even ending a sentence with a preposition is enough to unnerve me. How then can I ever expect to commit murder?

I must find some other way to deal the scuba diver.

As always, I need help.

I run from the room, screaming: "Nurse! Nurse!" There are no nurses in the vicinity (except for a dead one sprawled on a gurney, but she is no help), so I sprint down the hallway toward the nurses' station.

The walls of the hallway are pink. They used to be orange. Touching the wall to my left, I find that it is sticky, like licked candy. The hallway is also much longer than it used to be: I can't see the end of it, in either direction. It is definitely not the same corridor that was here before. Somehow, my wife's room must have moved to a different part of the building while I was busy with the scuba diver. Or maybe my wife's room remained stationary and the hospital shifted around it...

How could this happen? Was it the work of some outside agency—a powerful and malevolent construction company, perhaps—or did the architecture move of its own volition?

The implications of the latter dip me in cool sweat.

Pink sticky walls...

"Nurse!" I shout. "Doctor!"

No answer but a cough from the fluorescent lights.

"Nurse! Doctor! Janitor!"

A trashcan rolls along the ceiling, spilling its contents onto the floor. It passes overhead, and I dodge its rain of dirty needles and excised organs by throwing myself through the nearest open doorway. (Beyond the doorway is a room, thankfully, and not the black void to which some doorways lead.) I land on my belly within the room, and the trashcan clatters past in the hall.

My breath takes a moment to return.

I hear a noise—*squish-squish*—and smell a pungent odor.

Raising myself from the floor, I behold the occupant of the room: a frail and hairless woman, small in her hospital bed, hooked to dozens of machines that beep and hiss around her like futuristic toys. A scuba diver fish-flops on top of the unconscious woman, his moist red-and-purple wetsuit going *squish-squish*, his air tanks leaking farts. His feet are big with blue webbing between the toes. His goggles are full of sand and walnut-sized crabs.

Usually I am not one to defend the honor of strangers, but this situation compels me to intervene. I approach the bed and clear my throat. "Scuba diver!" I shout. "Cease what you are doing! Can't you see that this woman is ill?"

The scuba diver doesn't respond. He continues his flopping unabated. I swing out at his flailing limbs and grasp a webbed foot. The foot comes off and I realize that it is not really a foot but a plastic swimfin.

And underneath the swimfin is another swimfin. I grab this second swimfin and pull it off to reveal a third swimfin...

After pulling one hundred and eleven swimfins from the scuba diver's foot, I run from the room, screaming: "Nurse! Nurse!"

But there are no nurses in the vicinity (the dead nurse on the gurney has decomposed into a puddle of grape jelly). There is no one in the pink hallway but me. The fluorescent lights burp and fart and bleed.

My brain is a slow clock that ticks and stops, ticks and stops.

A trashcan rolls along the wall.

Running up and down the hallway, I open doors at random. In every room, the same scene assaults me: a comatose woman in a hospital bed with a scuba diver flopping on top. Five rooms, twenty rooms, one hundred rooms—identical misdeeds.

I vomit into a passing trashcan, wipe my chin, and sprint back to my wife's room carrying a lit stick of dynamite. The dynamite is cherry red. Its fuse hisses and throws off sparks that turn into fireflies as they float away.

My sanity, so long the oppressor, closes its eyes.

(Does it first wink?)

"Scuba diver!" I say as I twirl into my wife's room. "I have something for you!"

I halt in the doorway.

My wife turns to face me.

She is no longer in her bed, standing instead in the center of the room amid all the discarded swimfins. The scuba diver hangs upside down from the ceiling like a caught fish. His torso is open, spilling intestines, and my wife is cherry red with blood.

A smile breaks through the gore on her face.

"What are you doing out of your coma?" I ask.

"Why did you put me in that coma?" she asks.

"You shouldn't ask that," I say.

She shrugs and turns back to the gutted scuba diver. In her hand is a giant pair of scissors. Surgical steel. She plunges the scissors into the scuba diver's chest cavity and snips his sternum in half. The pattern on her hospital gown goes little duck, big dog, mushroom cloud, little duck, big dog, mushroom cloud.

My wife nods at the lit stick of dynamite in my hand. "What's that for?"

I look at the dynamite. "I... forget..."

The dynamite is sticky like licked candy.

I notice that my wife is wearing swimfins.

She spread-eagles the scuba diver's bisected rib cage

and reaches between his moth-wing lungs. She pulls out his heart, which is a tomato. She bites the tomato and its juice swirls into her eyes, which are marbles.

In my hand, the dynamite is about to explode, its fuse burned short. My wife, still chewing tomato, reaches over with her giant scissors and snips the fuse. The burning segment falls to the floor, fizzles out, and resembles a pubic hair.

Robbed of fire, the stock of explosive is impotent. I let go of it, and it falls up to the ceiling and rolls away.

"You look tired," my wife says. "You should lie down."

She is wiser than she knows...

I take off my shoes and crawl into her vacant hospital bed. The sheets are thin, wet with spit. The pillow is not a pillow but a chemistry textbook in a pillowcase.

My wife watches as I curl into her bed. My eyelids close and glue themselves shut. Something large and wet and web-footed flops like a fish on top of me.

The scent of flowers covered in dung.

My brain is a slow clock that ticks and stops.

Ticks.

And.

Stops.

LIGHT AMPLIFICATION BY STIMULATED EMISSION OF RADIATION

I want everything, but what I want the most is to fix my eyes. I have been abysmally myopic since prepubescence. As a child I often mistook my mother for a columnar puff of cotton. The human face resembled wads of rotting ham, and cityscapes were a dabbed patchwork of matte greasepaint. The hands of my little girlfriend bobbed in the air like huge translucent shrimp from the ocean bottom. I could never read the storybooks my friends were swearing by.

To see a thing clearly, it had to be a millimeter from my eye. Exactly a millimeter. As a boy I would sit for hours with some small trinket held just so—a pebble or breadcrumb or beetle—marveling at the sharpness and nuance of life in focus. The practice gave me headaches, daily. I coexisted with the headaches, the way a feral child can feel the freezing cold and not think it into a torture; it was only later, once my parents really got a hold of me, that I learned a headache was something to be hated. And so I stopped the practice of bringing things into focus.

I got glasses when I was ten. I wonder why it took so long. The lenses were five inches thick, the circumference of dinner plates. Their weight necessitated a complex system of scaffolding—a polyhedral cage of girders and wires encircling my head like an antique diving helmet modeled on the skull of a (demonically large) housefly. I could never figure out how to take the thing off. I slept in it, bathed in it. A small door in front allowed me to eat. But I rarely ate. Once a day I slurped some curdled milk through a long straw, and that was it. My body grew thin, a burnt matchstick bent beneath the massive metallic seed head of my glasses.

I passed puberty. I passed my exams, graduated high school, turned down an invitation to a pizza party (it would have been my first), and went to computer programming boot camp. Now I write code on a typewriter and get paid biweekly. I sit on a metal folding chair in my cubicle of rough particle board. I sweat inside my insectile helmet, staring out through its portholes at a world warped almost into true. My eyes have withered into dingleberries.

A boy brings newspapers to our cubicles. I never read mine. But I do collect the coupons from them. The coupons masquerade as obituaries. I think I'm the only one who knows about them. Everyone else thinks the obituaries are just obituaries. Could be the coupons are encoded holographically—latent in the surface text—and only certain eyes can reconstruct them. Eyes like mine.

I have enough coupons for a free bicycle. Or for two free unicycles. Or for half a canoe, or two sessions with a (demonically large) masseuse, or one fifty-slot toaster, or fifty rides on any roller coaster at Woe World. And those are all things I want—I want everything—but none of them are what I want the most. So I'm waiting. Saving more coupons. I almost have enough. If only more people would die.

The code I've been writing at work, it has something to do with lasers. We've been on this project for five years. It gives me headaches.

One day a school bus floods with gastric acid, digesting the children inside. Killing them. They appear in next week's paper as obituaries. Hundreds of them. (It was a very *long* school bus.)

I have enough coupons now.

I leave work early—sneaking out of my cubicle, taking the stairs down to the street—clutching my briefcase to my chest. My briefcase full of obituaries.

My briefcase is a plastic shopping bag.

On the street, I blink. Blink. Blink. The street shimmers; it bubbles and crawls, as if made of chameleons. My breath is loud inside the cage of my glasses. I walk downhill, away from the sun. A parade comes up the street. It swallows me. I emerge from its anus. Feral children follow behind it, dragging blocks of ice. I blink. Downhill. I am skeletal and shriveled; my eyes are dingleberries. I trip on a chameleon—fall to the sidewalk—roll downhill. Like a bouncing ball. A goalie stops me from entering his net; he deflects me into an alley, where an open doorway swallows me. My screams are loud inside the cage of my glasses. I blink, and the huge steel fishbowl on my head blinks with me. I am somewhere cold and sunless.

A doctor's office.

I am exactly where I meant to be.

I examine my briefcase. The plastic shopping bag is ripped in several places, obituaries sticking out—but none lost.

The receptionist tells me to sign in. I do. She waits two seconds, then calls my name. She says, "Why are you here?"

Too profound a question. I lift my briefcase to display the obituaries spilling out of it. I'm here to be seen. It's raining inside the cell around my head. I'm here to get what I want the most. To get it for free. I want the receptionist to receive me into a lighter world. I hope she has the eyes to see things my way. To see them free from their seeming flatness. I hope she doesn't think the obituaries are just obituaries.

She looks at me. She is like my mother, or like the little

girlfriend of my prepubescence, or like my single female coworker. She takes one of the obituaries, looks it over. It's a little boy's. Ian McCartney, age 9, biochemistry major (minor in holography) at Our Lady of Sorrows Elementary School. One of those who died in the very *long* school bus. In his picture, his face is ham.

The receptionist hands back the obituary, glances at my briefcase full of them, says, "Looks like you have enough for the free surgery. That why you're here?"

I nod. Yes! Nodding, my glasses bounce, their structure like a giant fossilized blowfish made of coat hangers and windowpanes.

The receptionist says, "The doctor will see you now."

She turns into the doctor.

"I see," she says, looking at the bear trap on my head. "You want to fix your eyes, don't you?"

Yes! Yes!

My glasses fill with rain. I open the small door in front, and water gushes out like words. It soaks the doctor, and she removes her shirt. Her nipples are eyeballs, then blocks of ice.

She says, "This should take no time at all." To make her statement literal, she pulls a gun and shoots the clock on the wall. The clock becomes a corpse, decomposes instantly. All moments occur at once, holographically superimposed. She says, "We have all the time in the world." No time; all time. She points the gun at me.

She fires a laser beam.

The laser passes unimpeded through my glasses. It hits my eyes. It shaves tissue from my corneas, reshaping them. Kissing my retinal flowers with photonic pollen.

Curing my myopia!

The doctor removes her pants. Her vagina is a wad of rotting ham. Her hands bob in the air like huge translucent shrimp from Venus.

I can't see!

Of course—I'm still wearing my glasses, making everything out of focus for my cured eyes.

I grab at the cage of my glasses, trying (like a million times before) to tear them off. For some reason I think it will work this time. It doesn't. My eyes (no longer dingleberries, after the surgery; blueberries, now) look out through the huge, heavy lenses at a world warped out of true. It gives me a headache.

I lunge at a shred of cotton that I take to be the doctor. I want to strangle her for doing this to me. The cotton sidesteps, and I fall to the floor. The doctor stands over me. I look up at the rotting ham of her vagina. It looks like my mother's face.

She says, "You still have coupons left. Enough for a free prosthesis."

And she fits me with a new pair of glasses.

The glasses fit over my old glasses, a second shell around the first. Each correcting for the other. With this addition, I can no longer lift my head. Immobilized on the floor. Anchored by a cancellation.

I have to get back to work. Surely my boss has noticed my absence by now. My typewriter sitting cold, a fragment of code abandoned on the page. Possibly my cubicle is glowing, as if irradiated, to alert of my desertion.

The doctor watches me writhe on the floor. She says, "We could fit you with a full-body prosthesis. To support the weight of your redundant augmentations. But, you have no coupons left."

I blink at her. My eyes are healthy blueberries buried in useless apparatus. This is not what I wanted.

"There is one special coupon you could use..."

No! I'm saving that one!

The doctor unhinges her jaw and vomits gastric acid on me. I struggle for an instant, then decompose, flying apart into countless laser beams. Folding back into flatness.

A boy brings the newspaper. The doctor takes it and flips to the obituaries. There I am. In my picture, my face is a (demonically large) eyeball. My obituary is very *long*.

The doctor clips it out. This special coupon is good for anything. Anything.

The doctor fits me with a full-body prosthesis to support the weight of my glasses. My empty glasses. The prosthesis hangs on empty space, a complex system of scaffolding encircling nothing. I'm nowhere. Because I'm nowhere, I'm everywhere, and because I'm everywhere, I'm a millimeter from everything. Exactly a millimeter.

All is in focus.

The full-body prosthesis gets up and goes back to work.

THE ASTROPHYSICIST, THE NEUROSURGEON, AND LUCIFER

The mother made a marionette out of cooked spaghetti and a roast chicken. She paraded the marionette in front of her son, manipulating the spaghetti to make the chicken lift its wing and wave hello. She made the chicken dance in midair, made it do vaudeville and slapstick. She did voices and made sound effects and watched her son's reaction, waiting for that smile she loved, the one that showed his molars and uvula.

"Mother," said the son, deadpan at the kitchen table, "is this art?"

He was forty-two years old and was an astrophysicist and neurosurgeon.

She looked into his mouth while he spoke and tried to see his molars and uvula. She was seventy-three years old and was once a famous chef—famous for presentation: for escargot dioramas and caviar mosaics and lobster animatronics and so on.

She made the chicken do Shakespeare, then karate. One of the strands of spaghetti snapped, and it was like the chicken had a stroke and lost function in its left wing, that side slumping toward the floor. The chicken was twelve weeks old at the time of death and eight months old at the time of defrosting.

"Enough presentation," said the son. "I want to eat."

"Not until you become a little boy again."

"Okay," he said, and picked up his fork and spoon and performed impromptu neurosurgery on himself, implanting stars and dark matter in the canyons of his forebrain. The dark matter was thirteen billion years old.

He became a little boy again.

She made the marionette pour a glass of white wine. She made it drink the glass of white wine. She made it pick up a knife and stab itself in the belly and carve open a hole there.

The hole was like a mouth that smiled, and it was that smile the son had been waiting for, that smile he loved— the one that showed the hollow pit inside the chicken, ribs and pelvis cradling the ice cubes that had formed from the white wine just imbibed. The son smiled like the hole; he was hungry, and he knew the moment of suicide was when the art turned back into food.

But the chicken went on with its act. It reached the knife across to its left wing, the one paralyzed by stroke, and hacked it off. It reached the knife up to its marionette strings and sliced at them, severing strand after strand of spaghetti—losing function all over its body. At last there was only one spaghetti string left, the one that controlled its knife-wielding limb, and this the chicken could not cut, impossible to reach (like licking your own uvula). It hung there from its last nerve, portrait of a stroke victim pending the final brushstroke.

The son said, "Enough presentation!" And he ran at the food.

His mother swung the chicken away from him. Ice cubes of white wine spilled from its open belly. The son stepped on an ice cube, and his feet slid out from under him. His skull hit the kitchen tile with a thunderclap.

He lost function all over his body.

He was a little boy again.

He lay there and watched the stars that reeled across the high kitchen ceiling. He watched his mother and her puppet. She was going on with the act, of course. Trying to, anyway. She moved the spaghetti strings, but their severed ends just flapped in midair. She let go of them, and they floated up to the ceiling. She held the one string left and watched the chicken swing at the end of it, her eyes getting dull; and a gnat flew away from her head with a microscopic ember clutched in its mandibles, and that was the last of her inspiration.

"We can eat now," she said.

But the son was watching the ceiling, the stars there and the strands of severed spaghetti that had floated up to them—the long and slimy spaghetti now winding among the stars, connecting them like lines charting the constellations. He saw a lobster constellation, a snail constellation. A fish, a bird, a cluster of grapes. He saw a woman, a wheat field.

He saw himself.

He was in the stars, a constellation. A man, not a little boy. An astrophysicist and neurosurgeon.

His star-self moved, its pasta contours wriggling. From its fingers there descended tendrils of spaghetti, long and wet and swaying as they lowered through the air.

The spaghetti strings burrowed into him. His star-self tugged, and the strings raised him up. He hung in midair, a little boy no more. The string moved that moved his hand, and he watched his hand move and knew that it moved in the now. In the present.

The present was zero seconds old.

The string moved that moved his mouth, and he said, "More presentation!"

His mother made a hollow sound. She stared down into the black and white kitchen tile, her body seeming to sink toward it. In one closed fist she still held the strand of spaghetti with the chicken on it, and as she sank, the bird sank with her, the sad mouth in its belly drooling out ice cubes of wine. The ice cubes hit the tile and melted there, forming a puddle; and at the edge of the puddle sat the gnat that had flown from her head, in its jaws the tiny ember that was her last spark, and the gnat sipped the wine and was drunk.

The mother had a stroke.

The son picked up his fork and spoon and performed impromptu neurosurgery on his mother. He poured white wine on her brain—a different year and vineyard than that the gnat was drinking; finer—and the gnat came buzzing to investigate. When it landed on the wine-soaked brain, the ember in its jaws tumbled loose and fell on the brain and ignited the fumes there (strong wine, to fume so) and set the brain on fire. Sparks like stars flew from the fire, turned to gnats in midair.

The mother smiled. The smile showed her uvula. (She had no molars; toothless with age.) She said, "Son, you are an artist."

He smiled.

The swarming gnats congregated into one body. The form of a man. Once a famous angel.

The morning star stroked his beard of gnats, looking on at the mother and son, at their young and hungry art. They met his gaze.

"Father," said the son.

IN CLOSETS HYPNOTIC

The doors opened and a junior businessman stepped inside. He pressed a button. The doors closed, and the elevator lurched into motion. The businessman straightened his bow tie.

A tall man wearing a trench coat stood in the rear of the elevator. He stared at the businessman, who was straightening his bow tie again and thinking himself alone.

"I'm Bob," said Bob. His trench coat was clean. "I am here."

The elevator stopped and the businessman got off.

The elevator dropped eighty floors. A couple stumbled aboard, groping and biting. They slammed into the far wall. A red-painted fingernail stabbed the button for a floor in the quadruple digits.

"I'm Bob," said Bob.

A pair of cashmere panties hit Bob in the face.

The elevator stopped and the couple got off. Rodin's *The Thinker* rolled in on a skateboard with a squeaky wheel. The Thinker failed to choose a floor. The elevator hung motionless, waiting.

"I'm Bob. What are you thinking about?"

The Thinker was silent.

"Are you thinking about what floor to choose? You can choose any of them. There are no limits." Bob lit a cigarette. "Try the basement."

JFK entered the elevator. He pressed fourteen buttons, all multiples of five or infinity. He said, "Hi, Bob."

The muzak system played the *Ride of the Valkyries* in a never-ending loop.

"Where are you headed, Bob?"

"Nowhere, really."

They came to the first stop. The doors opened and an elite techno-soldier somersaulted in. The soldier landed in a frog-squat on *The Thinker*'s head, threw open a hatch in the ceiling, and sprung into the darkness above, a hardback copy of Tom Clancy's *Rainbow Six* falling from his pocket and hitting Bob in the face.

Bob said, "I've been riding the elevator for seven days."

"Elevators," JFK said. "An enigma. You step into a closet, stand in a hypnotic trance for however long, and emerge from the closet into a new world."

They lapsed into silence while the elevator made its next ten stops, the doors opening to reveal: a hallway lined with fruit stands; a granite lobby with nine fountains; a brick wall; a police shootout; a mirror; Mount Kilimanjaro; the scene from *Goodfellas* where Joe Pesci gets whacked; nothing; nothing; Ragnarök.

Bob lit a cigarette and studied the figures that formed in the smoke.

The doors opened. Bob's mother stood in the hall, young and naked. *The Thinker* rolled out of the elevator. JFK followed. Bob's mother cupped her hand on *The Thinker*'s bronze buttocks. She kissed JFK's bicep. They entered a red closet and shut the door.

The elevator dropped five hundred floors, and Bob's true love got on.

"I love you," Bob said.

Bob's true love morphed into a senior businessman.

The elevator went up. It rocketed out of the atmosphere. The doors opened. Beyond them, white light roared mutely.

"I need those figures by noon," the businessmen said, and got off.

Bob said, "The figures." His flesh smoked as he morphed into a junior businessman. Figures formed in the smoke.

The figures. They added up to something.

"I am here," he said, and emerged into a new world.

He went to work.

GOODFeLLas

Taxidriver ran the stoplight. He almost got t-boned by an Oscar Mayer Wienermobile. Almost. Seconds later a police cruiser squawked its siren and swung into pursuit. Seeing the cop in his rearview mirror, Taxidriver laughed. His teeth were filthy.

In the backseat, Ragingbull was gluing sandpaper to his boxing gloves. When he heard the siren, he said, "Shit," and he threw more money at Taxidriver and told him to go faster.

Taxidriver was mentally ill. He went faster.

They outran the cop and arrived at their destination. Ragingbull jumped out of the car. He rushed into the building and busted through a door on the third floor.

Angelheart shrieked. She pushed Deerhunter off of her and scrambled beneath the bed sheets. Deerhunter roared like a primitive beast. He had been just about to climax, almost there. Almost.

"I knew it!" Ragingbull screamed. He stalked toward them, raising his boxing gloves.

Outside, Taxidriver kept the meter rolling. Twenty minutes passed and Ragingbull came stumbling out of the building. He was covered in blood and celluloid.

"Where to now?" Taxidriver asked.

"New York, New York. Cape Fear. Brazil."

a False and Hollow Word

The dictionary salesman opened his briefcase and pulled out a gun. He aimed the gun at the pilot's head and pulled the trigger. What shot from the barrel was not a bullet but a word, big blocky font that emerged one letter at a time like a scrolling headline... the word ONOMATOPOEIA traveling faster than sound toward the pilot's head...

The word struck the pilot's temple and bounced off with a heavy clang, falling dead to the dusty ground. The pilot adjusted his hat and grunted. The dictionary salesman reloaded, firing an ANTIDISESTABLISHMENTARIANISM at the pilot's head. The word bounced off the pilot's temple and crashed to the ground twenty-three feet below.

The pilot held onto one of the giant ribs that surrounded him, trying to move the rib like a lever. He peered ahead through the framework of bones. He made jet-engine sounds with his lips.

The dictionary salesman had parachuted in fifteen minutes ago. Word'd come from above that a Potential Buyer was alone and unarmed in the Really Dry Desert, and he, Salesman #788, had been chosen for the honorable task of dropping from the sky to accost the PB with his sales pitch of Words And Their Meanings Together In One Place For One Low Cost.

The pilot sat within the skeleton of a giant whale, up high and toward the front, the kind of dorsal-anterior place where you'd expect to find the creature's cockpit. The whale had been of the winged variety. The brittle cartilaginous remains of its flight appendages lay dormant against the yellow desert floor. Moldering scraps of cloth lay scattered among the bleached bones.

The pilot, high in his cockpit of bone, pretended to fly the whale skeleton. After his airdrop, Salesman #788 had climbed up into the skeleton, tombstone-like dictionaries dangling from his ankles, where they were secured with lengths of black chain. "Words And Their Meanings Together..." was as far as he'd gotten into his sales pitch before the pilot started shrieking. The sudden shrieks made Salesman #788 jump, drop the brochure he was holding, and nearly topple over backward off the skeleton. The pilot's shrieks revealed themselves as words:

"Impermeable cumulus ahead! A brick wall stretching across the sky! More altitude, MORE ALTITUDE! This is not a drill! This is war! The moment of truth! More altitude!" He turned a solid-blue eye to Salesman #788. "Peter, man your station!"

"Right away," Salesman #788 said, jumping into the copilot's seat and strapping in, donning his circuitry-laden helmet and lowering the oxygen mask over his mouth. He could taste the adrenaline in his esophagus. The Captain was right: This was the moment of truth. All their training had led to this. Do or die. Definitely not a drill.

"Bravery, Peter!" the Captain shrieked. "Courage!"

Another wave rocked the ship. Peter held the harpoon ready. They moved in tightening circles toward the center of the white-foam vortex, the ship creaking with doom. The Captain clopped across the deck, shouting orders to the various plates of inanimate food that made up the crew.

Mutiny from the spaghetti and meatballs, who claimed that the Captain's orders (Shred the sails! Load the cannons with oatmeal!) were counterproductive. After an unsuccessful revolt, the spaghetti and meatballs, the egg salad sandwich, and the meatloaf were forced to walk the plank and drop into the waters below.

Finally they approached the heart of the whirlpool, and Peter saw the giant eye that rested at the vortex's bottom. He flung the harpoon. An insane shriek sounded from everywhere at once as the harpoon shattered the eye's great corrective lens and continued on through the pupil, into the darkness within.

The Capt., ecstatic: "Ia! Ia!"

Peter was vaguely aware of a weight that seemed to pull at his legs, as if something large, heavy and filled with knowledge was chained to his ankles with lengths of black chain. The sea-monster vomited a cumulus cloud as it died. But the ship could not escape the force of the whirlpool: It careened downward into spiraling, watery darkness.

"We can survive this!" the Capt. yelled over the crash of the waves. He appeared to have grown younger. "Quick, switch me seats!"

Peter #788 switched seats with the Capt., a vertiginous wobble in his steps, as if he were on a tightrope across the thin beam of a bone, vertebrae an arch overhead, a parabola with sun as the focus, the horizon a granular directrix... earth upside down.

"Sir," said Peter #788, "can you define 'survive'?"

"Quick, switch me seats!"

The darkness was a desert.

"Quick, switch me seats!"

A dead whale at the bottom of the sea.

Peter #788 was both shocked and honored when the Capt. stood to announce that he, the Capt., was retiring and bequeathing his honorable title to Peter #788. Cobwebs stretched and broke as the Capt. removed his hat and slapped it down onto P788's head. Adjusting his new hat, the Captain #788 said, "But what will you do now? Flying was your life..."

"I was thinking of going into sales," said his copilot, who stood and grew a parachute out of his back. He lifted his legs—both of them at once—to display the tombstone-like dictionaries dangling there by their lengths of black chain. He said, "May I interest you in this special offer of Words And Their Meanings Together In One Place For One Low Cost...?" But the Pilot #788 barely heard him. He was too concerned by a bank of cumuli ahead to pay much attention to anything. He pulled a lever, trying to gain altitude. He hardly noticed the dictionary salesman standing beside him. He was only vaguely aware of a sensation in his legs like the absence of a mighty weight, as if some heavy thing had been chained there but was now gone.

The dictionary salesman recalled his training: In the Event of PBR (Potential-Buyer Resistance), Shoot to Kill.

So, in the present tense, the dictionary salesman opens his emergency briefcase and removes his gun and shoots the pilot with a word... the word NIHILCYCLICAL, which he's not even sure is a real word. He would look it up, but he doesn't own a dictionary.

The word bounces off the pilot's temple.

Salesman #789 fires again. And again. The words bounce off the pilot's temple, drop to the desert floor.

Salesman #789 scratches his nose and wonders what to do next when a cold wind rushes down and fills the parachute that had sprouted from his back, yanking him upward into the huge and terrifying sky. Far below, the pilot recedes, a young man growing old, the scraps of some abandoned uniform falling in shreds from his body.

very cold, very cozy

Adam missed his mother and decided to pay her a visit. He looked at the clock. It was midnight. Perfect. He packed a bag (flashlight, shovel, a snack) and left by way of the fire escape (something about the front door just then seemed vulgar).

The cemetery was ten precincts distant, but Adam knew a shortcut through the sewers—there was a boat, a chitinous oarsman, space distortion... ten cents to ride. He was there in no time, slightly dizzy and with the odor of exploded fireworks about him. He waded into the sea of tombstones, found the grave he wanted, and started to dig.

Only a foot or so of the digging was through grass and dirt. After that, the grass and dirt gave way to packing peanuts. Adam shoveled them out of the deepening hole, stopping to eat only a few. Eventually his shovel struck the lid of a coffin, and he bent to finish the job by hand, sweeping away what remained of the foam peanuts (eating just a few more).

The coffin was pink and had stickers of punk bands on it. Adam opened it, careful not to make a sound. Inside, pink bed sheets lay humped over a sleeping form, silver hair emerging up top to spill across a pink pillow.

"Hi, Mom," Adam said. He fell silent for a while. Then: "I miss you." He was whispering, not wanting to wake her. "I just thought I'd pay you a visit." The way she had the blankets cocooned around her, it was the way someone slept who was very cold, very cozy. "Well, I guess I'll get going now." He reached a hand toward her silver hair, wanting just a brief caress.

The hair was a wig.

The wig did not surprise him—he had known it was a wig, the same one his mother had worn throughout the hairless finale of her life. What surprised him was that there was no head beneath the wig. He lifted the heap of silver hair and found only the pink pillow, empty.

He tore back the sheets. A mound of clothes lay heaped up to suggest the shape of a body. The wig had been artfully placed to complete the illusion. It was like something a teenager would do to fool a parent.

Adam heard giggling. Then voices. They were muffled, almost inaudible. There was more giggling, also muffled. Some kind of gasp or moan. The noise was coming from somewhere nearby. From somewhere underground.

He knew what was going on here.

His parents had adjacent plots. The next grave over belonged to his father. That was where the noise was coming from. The giggling. They were over there together, stuffed scandalously into a single coffin. Giggling underground.

Giggling, gasping, moaning.

Adam jammed his fingers into his ears. He didn't want to listen, didn't want to endure the visions that listening would bring. He looked at the silver wig lying where he had dropped it. Maggots twisted within its depths.

His parents got louder. He started to hum.

In the wig, some of the maggots were becoming flies. The transformation was instantaneous, like popcorn exploding from the kernel. Adam thought of the chitinous oarsman in the sewer, whose eyes were like those of a fly. He felt dizzy again. His stomach churned, sick with the weight of packing peanuts (even though he'd eaten just a few).

Okay, okay—he'd eaten almost all of them.

The silver wig was now swollen with flies. It rose into the air, buoyed up by the fat black insects as they jittered into flight.

The wig dived at Adam.

He flung himself to the side, trying to dodge the attacking wig, but there was not much space for maneuvering in the open grave. The wig landed on his head. Pain swept across his scalp. He screamed.

Then the pain was over, only a dull burn left in its wake. The flies exited the wig en masse, a buzzing cloud that streamed away into the night. Adam reached up and yanked on the wig, trying to dislodge it. No use. The flies had stitched the wig into place, using their tiny limbs to knot things on a cellular level. It was part of him now.

He no longer heard any noise from his parents. They must have finished while the wig was attacking him. Probably they were cuddling now.

He waited.

When his mother finally snuck back into her own coffin, Adam did not confront her. He watched as she slid beneath the bed sheets and put her head on the pillow. She gathered the blankets around her, burrowing in.

Adam said, "Mom, we have to talk."

She ignored him. She was still, as still as if she had never moved at all. Adam waited. He scratched at the silver wig on his head.

He heard an infant cry.

The cry came from inside his mother. He pulled the bedding from her and saw that her belly was swollen. As he watched, it swelled even more. It grew so big that he had to back away from it. The skin stretched until it was translucent. He could see the unborn child inside. But it wasn't a child.

It was Adam.

He knew what was going on here.

His mother popped like a soap bubble. The explosion killed him with its concussive force, and he fell into the open coffin where his mother had just been. His body sank through the blankets, becoming cocooned within them. His silver hair spilled across the pink pillow.

The coffin lid swung shut.

Beyond the lip of the open grave, a naked man lay gasping for breath. It was Adam—the new Adam, fresh from the womb. He had been thrown clear of the grave by the force of the explosion. Now the world was upon him like a fist. He crawled to the edge of the grave and stared down at the pink coffin covered in stickers of punk bands. He had a brief vision of himself inside the coffin, himself with silver hair. Cold. Cozy.

He felt sick.

He vomited packing peanuts. Endlessly. The foam peanuts poured into the open grave, filling it. By the time he finished vomiting, there was only a foot or so of space left at top. He pushed loose earth into the remaining space, then finished the job with clods of grass.

He thought about going home. Home was ten precincts distant. He knew a shortcut through the sewers, but it cost ten cents to ride, and he had no money. He had nothing. He would have to walk home, naked in the night. He would climb the fire escape to his window, go in, and sleep for a long time.

He was so sick of being born.

MY EXTREMELY HORRIFIC CHILDHOOD

One time I was writhing on the ground near a busy intersection, and people kept stopping to ask if I was all right. I assured them I was, and after a final concerned glance, they went their way and left me alone.

One person who checked on me, his name was Crispy. He came up and sat down next to me, asking if I had a moment to talk. He was young—my age. He wore glasses and his hair looked neglected. He was smoking a cigarette, and I thought of asking him for one, but I had quit smoking. His upbeat demeanor annoyed me at first. He liked to talk. He was a Buddhist and a "certified counselor." He had created his own religion, a mash-up of Eastern philosophy, Christianity, and quantum mechanical chaos theory. He had hacked a satellite using a Tesla coil.

His real name was Christopher Pachelbel—hence, Chris P. Crispy.

He told me this story:

Where he grew up, slum housing in Chicago, the Halloween tradition was for all the tenement children to roam the halls and beg candy from each apartment. The building was so large and so populous that the children could trick-or-treat indoors the entire evening, never having to step foot outside. And with its orange wallpaper and black mold growing everywhere, with its spiders and rats and occasional human skeleton, the building was already perfectly decorated for the holiday.

Most of the families were too poor to afford costumes, so they had to improvise. Some of the costumes Crispy had worn throughout his trick-or-treating career were: a skull mask made of chewed gum; a big Santa beard made of soap bubbles; a mummy suit made of police tape; and a straightjacket made of a straightjacket.

The year in question, Crispy's costume was a bologna sandwich tied to his face with holes poked in it for eyes and mouth. His mother, putting the costume together, said, "This is smart because, once you get done wearing it, you can eat it." She was always finding ways to repurpose things, to get more from less. "All it takes is a little imagination," she said. He stared out at her through the eyeholes in the sandwich, and she stared back. "We're gonna make it, Christopher. Everything will be all right. I promise."

Crispy went one floor up to rendezvous with Monster, his best friend. Monster had a brown paper grocery bag over his head, holes in it for eyes and mouth, with the words FUCK YOU scrawled across the front in fat black marker. It was the same costume he wore every year. His mother had made it for him his first Halloween, and she just didn't give a shit.

"I'm a closet homosexual in a motorcycle gang," Monster said. Because his costume was nothing, he used it as a blank slate onto which he could project whatever he wanted. He came up with something new every year. Last year he was a dolphin researcher with "questionable ethics" and "a penchant for humiliation."

"Cool," Crispy said, playing along. "I'm a bologna sandwich, I guess." He shrugged. "I'm tomorrow's lunch."

"I bet you taste good, Crispy. I bet you're the best bologna sandwich anyone's ever had." Monster punched him in the shoulder. "And I bet I get more candy than you do!"

They started on the top floor and worked their way down. The first place they stopped, they met an enormous woman hooked up to eight IV poles. She gave them dead batteries. They thanked her and moved on. They got bottle caps, bits of string, cigarette butts. All the standard fare. A few places had rarer treats—packing peanuts, wet coffee grounds, finished crosswords—and the kids all swapped info as they passed in the halls, saying how there was shoe polish at 12D, how 23E had wads of greasy tinfoil, how there had been paperclips at 42F but they were all gone now. Crispy and Monster listened in, breathless.

One lead they got was: 9C.

That was way down from where they were, but they heard the apartment number repeated so many times, in such a hush of wonder, that they had to skip all the intervening floors and get there as soon as possible. They took the stairs in great leaps and slid down the railings and sometimes just free-fell through the empty air. A silent terror filled their hearts, that whatever was at 9C would be gone before they made it. They didn't even know what was there, exactly, only that it must be great. The other kids never said what kind of candy, just gave the apartment number and spoke no further.

Crispy had to hold his bologna sandwich mask in place as he rushed down the stairs, and Monster had to keep readjusting his brown paper grocery bag so that the eyeholes and the FUCK YOU were in position. A lot of candy bounced loose from their sacks, but they hardly cared. It was all rubbish, the same soiled napkins and toenail clippings they got every year. They had only ever pretended to relish such crap, while all along the facts had sickened and emptied them and they relished nothing. Such good pretenders, though.

They finally reached the floor 9C was on. They came bursting out of the stairwell, expecting the hall to be packed with trick-or-treaters, other kids all streaming away from 9C with the last of its treasure in their sacks. But there was no one. There was a cat. The lights flickered and a TV played behind one of the doors. Then even the cat left.

Crispy knocked on the door of 9C.

Monster whispered that he was scared. "And I don't know why."

Crispy thought maybe Monster was just afraid of greatness. But he didn't say that. He didn't say, "There is greatness behind this door, and you fear it," but that was what he thought, and he didn't know why. All he knew was that when the other kids had mentioned 9C, their eyes had turned to pinwheels.

The door opened.

A man stood there with a BLT on his face.

There were eyeholes poked in the sandwich, and the eyes that stared out of them were big and blue and bloodshot. There was an opening for the mouth, and the mouth was as big as a watermelon slice, and although the opening was actually smaller than the mouth, the entire watermelon slice still showed through somehow, like the sun caught in a pinhole. Little nubs of teeth glowed within the mouth, almost without order, a scatter plot of bone chips. A tongue lolled around in there, touching the teeth and lips absently.

The big blue eyes fixed Crispy and Monster in an unwavering gaze. The man said nothing and did not move from his doorway. Beyond him, his apartment was in darkness, but there were sounds, clicks and gurgles and inhalations and maybe a waterfall.

Crispy straightened his bologna sandwich mask and said, "Trick or treat."

Monster said it too. They held out their sacks.

And the man with the BLT on his face started to cackle and lunged at them and hooked their shoulders with giant hands and pulled them into 9C and shut the door.

Crispy thrashed around in the dark, screaming for Monster. He punched and kicked the air, but the man had let go and moved off into the darkness, his cackling seeming to come from everywhere. Crispy choked on the scent of bacon, lettuce, and tomato. He screamed again for Monster.

The lights came on.

The lights were candles made of bacon fat, endless candles all igniting at once and on their own. They illuminated an apartment that was half laboratory and half abattoir. A network of creaky gears ran throughout the confusing space, and chains and bellows and gauges and basins and cages and cauldrons and maps and flowcharts roamed everywhere. That was the laboratory part. The abattoir part was the blood splashed on every surface, the intestines piled wherever there was room, the sticks of bone, the wet lungs and livers and kidneys that lay like fallen petals on the floor.

Crispy spun around, trying to process the moment. He looked for Monster. He looked for the man with the BLT on his face. He looked for a weapon. He looked for the door. He looked, but not necessarily in that order, or in any order at all, just looking for everything all at once and thus finding nothing.

He realized he was still holding his sack of candy. He dropped it, and it spilled its contents across the floor, and its contents were chocolate bars and licorice and gumdrops and caramel, not bottle caps and cigarette butts and all the usual. He stared at the candy, feeling something stir in an undiscovered part of him. His heart squeezed tears up to his eyes, and the tears rolled out and fell and were reabsorbed.

"Monster!" He wanted Monster to see the candy. "Monster, look!"

The candles fluttered and a shape detached from the gory workshop and tackled Crispy, pinning him to the floor. He screamed and thrashed, but the man was heavy and strong, and the BLT smiled its watermelon slice.

The watermelon slice said, "Look!"

And the man swung an arm around to point at something. Crispy followed the finger but took a moment to see what was there.

It was a brown paper grocery bag, holes in it for eyes and mouth, with the words FUCK YOU scrawled across the front in fat black marker. It hung from a hook in the ceiling, open end down, and a spine stuck out the bottom, raw and red and dripping, freshly torn from its young body. The bag was wet around the mouth-hole from all the slobber that oozed off the swollen tongue of the head inside. The spine looked like barbecue.

"In the dark!" the BLT screeched, excited. "That's when I did it, in the dark, real quick before the lights came on. Real quick!" He cackled. He had Crispy beneath him, and he leaned in closer and said, "You don't have to worry. I won't do it to you. Just to the others. Not you. You're like me!"

His face jiggled, and globs of mayonnaise seeped out the edges and fell on Crispy. Some of the mayonnaise landed in his mouth, and he gagged. It tasted bitter. It was full of microscopic tadpoles. He spat it out. The bologna sandwich on his face was soggy with sweat, tears, and spittle, and he wanted to tear it away, to have his own face back. But the sandwich mask was the only thing saving him from the BLT man. And anyway, he couldn't get his arms free to do anything.

The BLT man laughed some more. His sandwich mask wasn't a mask, of course. Its ingredients glistened like animate tissue. He pointed at his face and said, through the laughter, "See, this is smart because, once you get done wearing it, you can eat it!" Ha-ha-ha-haha! "We're gonna make it, Crispy! Everything will be all right. I promise!"

Crispy got an arm free. He clawed at the man's face, opening furrows in the bread. Blood gushed. The man screamed and fell backward, and Crispy rolled away and jumped to his feet and ran, slipping on guts and crashing into tables full of glass and metal. He tore through the jungle of equipment, seeking the door. His hand ripped a hanging from the wall—an actual-size anatomical drawing of a human child—and there was the door.

Crispy burst through it. He ran, ran, and ran, down the hall and up the stairs, not looking back. He heard cackling in his head.

He rushed home and tried to tell his mother what had happened. But the story got stuck inside of him, too huge for his tongue to carry. She seemed not to notice his terror and exhaustion. She asked if he had fun. Then she told him to take his mask off and eat it, that that was his dinner, and she smiled again at her resourcefulness, at her imagination that made do with the facts. Hidden uses, yes, and one thing could be two. They were going to make it.

Because it made his mother happy, Crispy ate his mask.

He ran into Monster the next day. They played in the hall, but not for very long. Monster was quiet, and sometimes his eyes turned into pinwheels. He smelled like bacon. From then on, whenever Crispy ran into him, which was not often, he always smelled like bacon. And so did a lot of the other kids.

This made Crispy different.

"So you see," he said as we sat there near that busy intersection and he smoked and I didn't, "I know what it's like. To be different." He told me where he lived and to stop by anytime, and then he left.

Had he really not recognized me? Of course we hadn't seen each other for years, not since we were kids and had grown apart. It was true what he said. I did smell like bacon all the time, and my eyes sometimes turned into pinwheels.

I started writhing on the ground again, but now no one stopped to ask if I was all right. I was invisible. I rolled into the intersection, and a car smashed me apart, my husk rupturing like an old melon and the insides spewing out, and the insides were bacon, lettuce, and tomato, and a bitter mayonnaise full of tadpoles.

peaches and cream

The boy felt sick. Something he ate. He stared at the table, not at the girl across from him. On his plate, whatever had made him sick—the half-eaten peas, the half-eaten ham, the half-eaten peaches and cream—was laughing silently at him. He pushed the plate aside.

The girl stabbed her fork into his peaches and cream. He wanted to warn her. She was too quick, already chewing... a dribble of cream turning clear on her lip...

Maybe it wasn't the peaches and cream, he hoped.

She made a face.

It was the peaches and cream.

The boy held his belly. He said, "It's not my fault. I'm sorry."

The girl stabbed her knife into her belly. She opened herself from pubis to sternum, reached in, and pulled out the bag of her stomach. She sliced the bag open; gastric juice poured out. She reached in, scooped out the peaches and cream, and started raking clean the walls, her long nails (painted red) scraping the tissue raw. She let the peaches and cream fall to the floor, where it landed in an unexplained dog bowl that was dirty.

"All better," she said, and put her voided stomach on the table. "The difference between you and me is, when I have an issue, I address it directly. I won't just sit and suffer."

The boy said, "Suffering is sweet!"

The girl passed out due to being disemboweled. Her face hit the table, right where her stomach was, and the stomach made a sound like a whoopee cushion. She was beautiful and empty.

Wincing in gastrointestinal distress, the boy slid off his seat, down to the floor. He pulled the dirty dog bowl close and lowered his face to it.

THE FAILED ROMANCE

The way you get fat without noticing, that's how I got pixelated. The realization came suddenly—wake up one day; look in the mirror; think, "Fuck, I'm pixelated!"—but I knew it had been happening for a while. I could even remember noticing it early on, in an absent, preconscious way. Thinking about this, I nearly had an insight into the nature of time and dying; but rather than finish the insight, I urinated into the toilet and blew my nose on two squares of toilet paper and mumbled the word *fuck* and thought about food and felt terror.

I came out of the bathroom, into the bedroom, and looked at my wife. She was reading in bed. She had her wedding dress on—hadn't taken it off since we got married seven years ago.

"Honey, do I look pixelated?"

She lowered her book. Her wedding dress, once white, was black with fungal filth. She said, "Maybe a little."

"Yeah, I thought so too."

I got into bed beside her and went to work.

"Went to work" sounds like some kind of innuendo for sex, especially after saying, "I got into bed beside her," but I don't mean it that way. I mean that I pulled my computer to me and started typing; I'm a programmer, and I work from home—usually propped up in bed beside my wife. I put a clothespin on my nose to keep from smelling the rot of her wedding dress. I can do this without offending her because I have a special-made clothespin that's invisible.

I looked at my code. There was a line that said: FAIL AS A MAN.

This line was—out of place. The line was out of line. It didn't even follow the syntax of the language I was writing in. I crossed my arms and stared at the screen. I wasn't sure how to go on.

Our neighbor walked into the bedroom without knocking. He thought it was funny to do that. There was a character on a sitcom that always did that—walked into his neighbor's apartment uninvited. Our neighbor wanted to be that sitcom character; he liked the sitcom character more than he liked himself. His life was not a story.

To get to our bedroom, the neighbor had to first come through the front door (after picking the lock), pass through the living room, pass through the dining room, leap the pit of wooden stakes, climb the stairs, and come down the hall. All this preliminary footwork made his "spontaneous" entry into our bedroom much less comical than the corresponding behavior of the sitcom character.

"Harry!" he spouted my name.

I ignored him, kept looking at my code. FAIL AS A MAN.

Our neighbor started going through our drawers. He took balled socks from the sock drawer and started juggling them. "Harry!"

My wife lowered her book and glared at the neighbor. She said, "Harry, do something."

I got up and defenestrated the neighbor.

I returned to bed. I sat and stared at my belly. My pixelated belly. The pixels were so huge that I could count them. I counted a baker's dozen (plus or minus a few as the resolution wavered). Fuck. Shit.

FAIL.

Envision a future where this just gets worse: my belly eventually just one huge pixel; my face a shapeless cake of squares.

Our neighbor walked in again. His legs were broken from when I threw him out the window, so he was walking on his hands. "Harry!"

I got up to confront him. I did a handstand so that our faces met. The blood that rushed to my head sounded like an airplane in a seashell. It was the first time in months that I'd been aware of my own circulation.

"Excuse me," I said to the neighbor, "but you are not a sitcom character. You are unremarkable and anonymous."

"And you," said the neighbor, "are pixelated."

I defenestrated him again.

When I got back into bed, my wife was asleep. Stiff mushrooms grew from the rot of her wedding dress. I picked one and ate it. I pulled my computer to me. I looked at the code on the screen. It said: FAIL AS A PROGRAMMER.

I defenestrated my computer.

I looked at my wife. Stared at her. Stared *hard*. Trying to see her anew. She was the daughter of Shanti-om-Shanti, a great warlord, and I had conquered hordes of Shantians to have her. I had soared through skies of brain, swum up rivers of blood, striven with monsters (both inner and outer), etc. Our courtship, though brief, was long with deeds: I painted portraits, penned letters, studied a tongue; I wrote computer programs that were actually elaborate poems to her; she composed ballads, made collages, mailed me bombs and dolls of hair; she drew maps to lead me to the riches of her limbic system. Our pheromones clouded half the globe, caustic as fallout; every mix CD I sent her was a lovingly crafted experiment in terror...

Seven years. The way you get fat without noticing, that's

how we forgot each other.

I picked another mushroom from her rotten wedding dress. I ate it. It tasted like egg. The book she'd been reading lay fallen beside her sleeping form. It was a fat paperback romance written in Unicode.

The neighbor returned, busting through the door rather than opening it. Now not only his legs were broken, but his arms were as well, from when I threw him out the window a second time—so instead of walking in on his feet, or walking in on his hands, he walked in on a set of mechanical spider legs.

He had my computer. He must have gotten it when I threw it out the window after him. The mechanical spider legs were connected to the computer; they *were* the computer: elegant appendages that had unfolded from within the machine's innards, sprouting like mutations.

I got a glimpse of the computer screen. The coding problem I'd been working on for weeks—it was solved. The neighbor must have cracked it while lying outside, broken arms keying in some graceful fix after just a momentary glance at the screen. There was no code telling him to FAIL AS A NEIGHBOR; instead, the screen played a porno involving two red brains. A cursor blinked in the upper right-hand corner... indicating consciousness...

He'd done it: completed the code, imbued the machine with a soul... a soul of roaring electrons—hyperaware on a subatomic level—in conscious control of its own nanotech structure... able, for instance, to sprout limbs at will: to form a cradle for the broken neighbor and be his monstrous legs...

The explosiveness of his entry awoke my wife. She saw him, cursed, threw her book at him. Earthworms had replaced some of the stitching on her wedding dress.

The neighbor—he was wearing the suit I got married in.

"Unremarkable?" he said, his digitized voice emerging

from the computer speakers. "Anonymous?"

My wife said, "Harry, do something!"

I did something: I got more pixelated.

Like someone spontaneously putting on three hundred pounds, I flashed forward to a state of morbid pixelation. I was one giant pixel.

I told my wife, "*You* do something!"

She was looking at my wedding suit on the neighbor. "You were so handsome, Harry," she said. "Why aren't you handsome anymore?"

"I'm older. I have more worries. I don't know."

She touched the edge of my pixel, as if stroking my cheek. "We have to do something..."

The neighbor was juggling socks again, dozens of balled pairs going at once on his spidery cyber-legs. Watching the socks revolve, I nearly had an insight into the nature of time and dying.

Rather than finish the insight, I said, "Let's renew our vows."

"And go on a second honeymoon," she said.

"Yes, to Hawaii," I said, naming off some imaginary state.

"I'll clean my dress," she said, scraping away a square of fungus to illustrate, "and dye my hair fuchsia."

"I'll wear my suit..."

My suit—the neighbor was not my size, and my suit fit poorly on him, seeming both too small and too big. Who knows, maybe that's how it would fit on me now, too. But, ill-fitting or not, it belonged on me—as rightly as my own skin... the suit symbolic of a second body I had assumed...

The neighbor juggled more and more socks, soon employing every pair in the drawer. Then he juggled the drawer itself. Then the dresser. Then the bed, tumbling us out of it. He was now juggling everything in the room, his spider legs a blur. The computer had sunk wires into his brain; he and it were one. A message appeared in the cyclone of juggled things, spelled out by the socks and hairbrushes and alarm clocks and Kleenex boxes: FAIL AS A HUSBAND.

I attacked the neighbor, leaping into the swarm of stuff that orbited him. In search of a weapon, I reached out and plucked something from the air at random. It was my wife's book—the fat paperback romance written in Unicode.

Wires snaked all over the neighbor, slithering in and out of his pores as my sentient computer merged with him further. Soon all I could see was his face, the rest of him wrapped in silvery techno-foliage, leaves of circuitry that climbed throughout the room like a sudden jungle. His face, even drowning in cyber-jungle, was unremarkable; he looked like my wife's father, the great warlord. He looked like me—before I was a pixel.

My wedding suit was somewhere in all that jungle.

I opened my wife's romance novel and started to read. The hexadecimal swirled on the page, blurring into a soup of possibility. The whole novel was like that. A primordial soup of potential romance.

She had been reading this book for seven years.

I looked around for her. But she was gone, swallowed by the jungle.

FAIL AS A HERO.

No. Keep reading. This romance—my "weapon"—had to be more than just a swarm of characters. Surely there was something sharp in it, something defined. A true story.

I pored over the book, dodging a dresser drawer that flew at me from the swarm of juggled furnishings. I dodged a lamp, an alarm clock, the bed. All while the romance still refused me.

The mirror from my wife's vanity crashed into my skull, and an egg of blood cracked open in my head. Suddenly I could read my wife's book.

It began: "You are in a jungle."

I was.

"You have a machete."

I did.

I raised the machete. Around me, the jungle had thickened to a mesh of digital static. I was part of it... a pixel in its empty signal...

I swung my machete.

The static cracked open. Through the opening, I saw my neighbor. I swung my machete at him. His skull cracked open; and through the opening, I saw the vacant set of a sitcom.

I sliced like wild all around me, cutting down the choking growth. Clearing the static. I saw my wife. The fungal colonies were falling from her dress, revealing the fabric underneath... the dress pure and new again—though not its original white: no, it had yellowed; but that was good, that was right. The yellow was a ripening, a slow and endless shading toward a deeper value... a new color coming constantly into its own...

My wife smiled. I smiled. Swung my machete. Laughed and spat as the tangle of digital flora fell away, pure sands and palm trees springing up in its place. A private beach. The shore a smooth analog curve.

My wife stroked my cheek. I could see my reflection in her eyes. I was in my wedding suit. If I was made of pixels, they were too small to see.

I said, "We are on an island."

We were.

She said, "We have each other."

We did.

We jumped out of the window.

SIGN HERE, AND HERE, AND HERE

"I need to eat to be happy. I need to eat souls like yours. I also like cold cuts and ice cubes. I am remorseless."

That was what the garbage disposal said to Ian on his third night in his new apartment. Two nights before, when he turned on the shower for the first time (he had neglected to check it before signing the lease), ground beef came out.

The tub drained into the apartment below, where a hungry man lived, but Ian ignored that. He called his landlord on a rotary phone, and when he put the receiver to his ear, ground beef came out.

"The cracks in the walls are a map. Have you any porridge to pour down here? Imitation grits?" Fingers reached up through the garbage disposal. Ian turned on the hot water, blistering hot, and hammered at the fingers with a giant spoon. He flicked the switch that worked the garbage disposal, but this only lowered a disco ball in the closet.

The fingers retreated back down the drain, and a mouth took their place. It had two rows of teeth. Ian remembered his landlord, the sole time they met. The man had been chewing bubblegum, the pink rubber strung between two rows of teeth. Ian had signed the lease.

The hungry man was his landlord.

"I must have comfort food," said the garbage disposal. "My food the comfort of others." Ian thought you could interpret that in two ways.

Maybe three.

He put a dirty plate over top of the drain.

Going for a beer, he remembered that the refrigerator was full of cake, every cubic inch of space, so that when he opened the door, it was just a wall of cake facing him. A wedding cake, to judge by its frosting.

The dirty plate on top of the drain was dirty with ketchup and soap suds.

Pissed at not having a beer, Ian went to his "office" and dug through his papers on the floor until he found his lease. He combed through it, trying to find some loophole out of this shit.

The lease said: "I agree to live in this shit for one (1) year and not complain. I agree to marry one (1) of your daughters and not complain. I, the undersigned, agree to live the Good Life and never, ever complain."

He had signed it.

She came up behind him, put the cold beer on his neck playfully. He winced at the chill, and she slid her arm around his shoulders. He took the beer from her and opened it with his teeth, of which he had two rows.

The bottle was full of ground beef.

She said, "How are you?"

He said, "I can't complain."

She suggested they shower. In the shower, he soaped her breasts, and the showerhead bled ketchup and cold cuts.

The hungry man in the apartment below screwed his mouth to the ceiling, sucking down what drained from their shower. He ate well—grew huge—filled his apartment, so that when you opened the door, it was just a wall of him facing you. A lonely man, to judge by his moaning.

DOUBLE CHIN

I woke up yesterday morning with a double chin. I cut the second chin off and fried it for breakfast. It was too fatty. It was all fat. I ate it with mustard. When I think I won't like the taste of something, I put mustard on it so that I'll taste just the mustard.

This morning I wake up with another double chin. I eat it for breakfast, thinking this chin might be better than the last. It is worse. I eat it with ketchup. I go to the doctor and ask why I keep waking up with double chins. He says, At least you have a reliable source of food. I say, My chins are too fatty for my tastes. He says, Fat is good for the heart, it insulates it. I say, I would rather eat my heart than my chin. He says, For heart insulation, fiberglass also works well. I say, It would probably take a lot of mayonnaise to make a heart taste good.

THE OLD MAN AND THE SEA

At the Comfort Inn in Toronto you say: I'm uncomfortable.

I adjust the cuffs around your wrists and ankles and adjust your blindfold and lower the voltage on the electrified nipple clamps. "Better?"

No. So I put headphones over your ears and play the sound of crashing ocean waves and gulls calling to their mates. Because I remember the time we went to the beach. The headphones block my voice, but I anticipated this and recorded myself speaking over the ocean sounds, a prefab convo with blanks left for you, so that we could continue to talk. Inaudible to me now, the mix of ocean and speech in your ears, but I remember my half completely.

"Better?" the headphones ask.

You: No, but the ocean is nice. I remember the time we went—

"Good, I'm glad. I want you to be comfortable." A gull screeches. "Just relax."

—sure, I will, but you remember that crab that scuttled out of the foamy tide, a black diamond in its claw, and came right at us? I was on my back with my legs up and a little apart, and it darted in and swept its feelers all over my buttocks and inner thighs and higher, grazing my—

"You say you're hungry? I'm a little hungry too. Let's get room service." The ocean booms, and in the darkness behind your blindfold you see shipwrecks in progress. "This budget inn is unique in that it offers such amenities, although the only thing on the menu is eggs."

I pick up the red telephone and dial the front desk and order seven fried eggs, and you neither see nor hear me do this.

"On its way," the headphones tell you. I recorded my lines in a calm, seductive voice, trying to sound like that narrator in movie previews. "After our midnight snack, how about we electrocute your nipples more intensely?" The gap for your response passes without you filling it, like you're drifting off or something. "For the last time, just *forget* about your father."

A knock on the door and it's room service: a compact septuagenarian in a black vest pushing a metal cart with a covered plate on it. Male, I can tell by the mustache—stiff grey bristles meticulously curled. He wheels into the room and uncovers the plate, and seven egg yolks reflect the picture (fuzzy, skipping) on the TV in the corner... an episode of *Three's Company* I've seen twice, nauseatingly overlaid with the film *The Driller Killer* that's airing, censored, on a nearby frequency...

"There's one egg missing," the headphones tell you, although there isn't.

"Please," says the septuagenarian, "I was wondering if maybe you could help me." He takes our plate of eggs off the cart and sets it on the bed beside your squirming legs, then reaches into the drawer of our nightstand and comes up with another plate, covered, which he puts where ours just was. "Could you deliver this to the next room over?"

"A little busy here."

"Do an old man a favor."

Fuck, that stock phrase obligates me. I grab the cart and push it out of the room, and as the door closes behind me, the "old man" smiles, his mustache falling off, and says to me, with a glance at you on the bed, "Don't worry, I'll take good

care of your friend here. Make sure they *tip* you over there."
Then the door clicks shut and I'm alone in the hallway in my
underwear (had been pantsless in the room with you) with
a metal cart that I push one room over, to the door with the
DO NOT DISTURB card hung on its handle.

I disturb.

The door swings open under my fist, room number
falling from its chintzy screw. The black ceramic numeral, a
seven, bounces off my foot... scuttles away across the carpet...

In the room, a body tied to the bed, blindfolded, headphones
on. In a chair pulled up to the bed sits a septuagenarian in a black
vest, without a mustache, eating fried eggs off a plate balanced
on the bound person's abs. Looking up: "Ah, my eggs, at last!"
Says it just as the old plate empties.

I wheel in and uncover the new plate. Six fried eggs.

I put the plate on the bed beside the squirming legs that
aren't yours, can't be, because you're one room over still, but
that look like yours in that they're cuffed to the bedposts and
attached to a body with the same scars. The septuagenarian
reaches under the bed, comes up with another plate, covered,
and says, "Please... could you... an old man..."

The body on the bed reacts as my voice over the
headphones barks something sudden and harsh, I can't
remember what (have lost my place in the script). I snatch
the plate from the aged hands and drop it onto the cart and
turn the cart around and wheel it out of the room, speed to
the next room over, where I knock rapidly. The door swings
open, room number falls, black ceramic, a six, scuttles away,
quick as a crab on legs I can't see, disappears beneath the bed.

On the bed, you.

No, not you. Same as in the last room, but here the bound
person has lost the headphones to the septuagenarian, and
the septuagenarian sits cross-legged on the bed rather than

in a chair beside it, eating fried eggs off a plate balanced on the bound person's face, mouth full while conversing with my voice heard through the headphones, my narrator voice with the ocean crashing in the background, an attempt to calm you, to comfort you, to seduce and communicate.

"I think I know a thing or two about *that*," says the "old man" in response to some statement (an empty truth, probably) that I recorded myself saying. Then, looking up: "Ah, my eggs!"

I uncover the plate.

Five eggs.

Now I know where we're at in the script. "Two are missing," the headphones say to the ancient in the black vest, although there aren't.

I put the plate on the bed.

And receive another.

Scurry in fast-forward to the next room over. Knock in fast-forward and the door explodes into fragments. The room number, a five, swoops off like a bat and burrows into the curtains. Fast-forward because I wanted this to be over with lifetimes ago, this service. Fast-forward because I have unfinished business with you. I uncover the plate, four eggs, and throw it at the compact septuagenarian crouched on the bound person's chest, catch the new plate that falls from the ceiling, and fast-forward out of there... to the next room...

Several rooms later I'm opening the door with an axe— first swing shattering the black ceramic numeral (a one) as I giggle. The plate I hold with the hand not holding the axe, it has zero eggs on it. Zero. The only thing on the menu.

And at the next room—its number an ouroboros—the plate holds a black diamond.

In the room, on the bed, a body tied up, the same as you, same scars, same scoliosis and torpor, but not you, no, despite the squirming legs banded with contusions from when I flogged them with my belt, despite the reluctance to feel good...

Okay, okay—it *is* you.

Nestled close to you on the bed, the "old man" in the black vest—female, I can tell by the lack of mustache—has gone pantsless. Your skulls are pressed together, the headphones stretched over both of them. The black diamond on the plate in my hand, it weighs as much as the ocean, so I put it down, not paying attention to where. Your mouths move in unison, hers toothless, yours full of a ball gag—red, like a yolk of blood—speaking, with these handicaps, into the gap I've left you, the window I left open to listen through, as if I could hear at all over the crash of waves, the screech of gulls, the fuzz of time.

You and her, you say: I feel a little hungry.

And her gnarled claw reaches down, to where your legs writhe, bound, up and a little apart, and the hand darts in and sweeps its orangey nails all over your buttocks and inner thighs and higher, all in fast-forward, grazing your genitals of indeterminate sex. The nails click shut around your sex as the ocean in your ears groans against the suck of a sudden divide, a schism cracking the seabed, and my voice—inaudible to me now, but I remember my half completely, even when I forget—comes over that tectonic groan, "You say you're hungry?" (*Grooooooan.*) "Let's get room service." And the hand with your severed genitals in it goes up to the mouth of the ancient servant, who eats them.

On the bedside table, the red telephone rings.

It's them again. Us.

I run to the TV and reach through its broken screen to the stack of covered plates within, the eggs you've been frying on your electrified chest. I grab the order of eight eggs and dash out of the room with it, sprint down the hall, cradling the delivery like a ball in some sport. I run past the open doors (open because I left them so) of all the rooms I just serviced, remembering: I forgot to get them to tip me. I don't stop, don't look inside, don't listen (screams, breathless pleas), don't feel—allow nothing, not until I make it to the end of the hall, back to our room. The only room with its door shut. DO NOT DISTURB.

I disturb.

I disturb with an axe.

Bursting through the splintered door, I shout your name. Your real name. But you are not in the room. Only the septuagenarian. She gets up off the bed, licking her lips from the meal just had. I stare at the empty cuffs where lately your legs had squirmed. A mustache scuttles across the carpet, finds the crusty foot of the ancient, and scales her body to her upper lip, where it settles into place.

The "old man" smiles. Says, "I *told* you I'd take good care of your friend." He sees the covered plate in my hands. "Ah, dessert!" He steps toward me, and suddenly the room erupts with the sound of an angry sea, the ringing of an empty voice, as the cord from the headphones pulls out of its jack in the stereo. My narrator voice, it sounds weak from talking so long, weak and losing strength, as if I'm drifting off or something, and I guess I don't remember this part.

It's saying: "—that crab that scuttled out of the foamy tide, a black diamond in its claw—?"

The old man takes his eggs.

I remember something.

"Please... a tip?"

He cups a hand and positions it under his buttocks, shits a black diamond into it, and with a small grin presents the diamond to me.

I take the tip. I stare through its facets. It's what's become of you.

And though I know it's poor service, I raise my axe and cut the old man down.

THE BALLOON ARTIST

The birthday boy lifted the AK-47 from its box. He grinned and said, "Thanks, Kevin!"

Kevin grinned back, chocolate cake smeared around his mouth like a larger mouth.

The birthday boy pointed his new AK-47 at the balloon artist. "Mother promised the best balloon artist in the world."

"I am the best in *all* worlds!"

"Prove it," the birthday boy said, and fired a warning shot into the ground.

The balloon artist yelped. He twisted a long slender balloon into the shape of an Old English Terrier. A pearl of sweat quivered at his temple as he presented the Old English Terrier for inspection.

Kevin sneered. "Not very realistic."

The birthday boy put a bullet in the balloon artist's kneecap. The balloon artist folded to the ground, allowed himself two seconds of terrified screaming, and then launched into the construction of another animal.

It was his greatest work ever: a life-sized zebra with functioning genitals and the brain of a philosopher-king. The zebra spoke, introducing itself as the Alpha and the Omega.

The birthday boy fired his AK-47 at the Alpha and the Omega.

The zebra thrashed, balloon organs exploding. Scraps of latex rained down to litter the earth, all trace of divine intelligence gone.

Kevin high-fived the birthday boy.

The balloon artist allowed himself three seconds of bereaved weeping—the Alpha! the Omega! murdered!—and then launched into the construction of, not a balloon animal, but a balloon weapon: an AK-47.

He squeezed the trigger, and the gun fired a barrage of sewing needles and lit cigarettes. A needle hit the birthday boy, and he popped like a balloon, his own AK-47 clattering to the ground. Kevin screamed, and then he too popped, pierced by the cherry of a cigarette.

The balloon artist swept gunfire through the birthday party. The guests popped, popped, popped. The cake (an enormous chocolate octopus) popped; the presents (pastel boxes that sweated and coughed) popped; the petting zoo (pygmy gorillas and defanged cobras in an enclosure of hay) popped. Scraps of false cheer rained down and turned to mud, all trace of the birthday party gone.

The balloon artist kept firing. In the distance, a stand of trees popped. A line of hills popped. Everything between him and the horizon—popped. He stood alone at the center of an empty plane.

His gun floated out of his hands, into the sky.

He tried for years to recreate his greatest work. He produced zebra after zebra, but none were the Alpha and the Omega. He rejected them, and they galloped away to start their own civilization.

UMBreLLa

A hairless man wearing aviator sunglasses dives into a swimming pool full of submarine sandwiches. He swims from one end of the pool to the other, doing the breaststroke through meat and veggies. A piece of rotten cheese clings to his shaved head.

After thirty minutes he emerges from the pool and stretches out on a bear-skin rug. A large-breasted woman wearing a barbed-wire bikini brings him a drink. The drink has an umbrella in it.

"Darling," says the woman, and she rubs his tan.

He lifts his aviator sunglasses. He smiles at her. He lowers the sunglasses back over his eyes and sips his drink.

There is a palm tree nearby. The sunshine is like something out of a music video. The man has music videos playing on the inside of his sunglasses, a different video on each lens. One of the music videos is highly pornographic.

"Son," says the woman, and she begins to knit.

The man lifts his sunglasses. He didn't notice before, but the large-breasted woman in the barbed-wire bikini is his mother.

His mother reaches over and peels the piece of cheese from his head.

He screams, jumps up from the bear-skin rug. He dives back into the pool full of submarine sandwiches and swims furiously to the other end, covering the entire distance of the pool in two seconds. He is still holding his drink with the umbrella in it.

His mother is waiting for him at the other end. She teleported there somehow. Perhaps knowing how to teleport is part of her maternal instinct. She stares down at him from poolside as he swims in place. He gazes up at her and wonders what to do.

An umbilical cord unravels from his mother's abdomen. It snakes through the air and lashes his chest like an alien tail. Then it coils itself around his neck and squeezes.

"No," the man gasps. His hands flail (the right hand still casually grips his drink). He tears open submarine sandwiches, looking for a weapon. In one sandwich he finds a long kitchen knife.

He swings the knife at the umbilical cord, severing it.

His first girlfriend steps out from behind his mother and approaches the edge of the pool. Her face has morphed into that of a cat.

"You stay away," the man shouts, wiggling the kitchen knife at her. The man is crying now. Every inch of him is greasy. He suddenly feels—old.

His first girlfriend extends a booted foot. She plants the foot on his head. He hacks at the foot with his knife. She presses down. He struggles to stay afloat but is still unwilling to relinquish his drink. His first girlfriend meows.

She pushes him beneath the surface. Her foot holds him there. He can't breathe. The foot pushes him deeper. And deeper. He sinks through fathoms of meat and cheese.

Things become different. The sandwiches disappear, giving way to something dark and blue and cold. There are bubbles, tiny and everywhere.

It is raining fish.

The man removes the umbrella from his drink and holds it above him. Fish thud off the umbrella and he wonders when he'll reach the bottom.

Carbon Dating Cold Feet

There are fifty people at the party and only two of them are dancing. I want to be the third. I feel my limbs whimper for release. My legs want to run in a circle with the circumference of myself. My torso wants to rotate along all three axes of familiar space, and along other axes. I want to dance.

I dance, a little.

But the vast magnetic arm loses its grip on me, or I lose my grip on it, and I fall back into the chill of constrained matter.

Of the two people dancing, one is a man in a bra.

I love him.

He came with a friend. The friend is now my friend as well, because we talked earlier. He keeps disappearing and reappearing. I think he goes outside often to pee on the burning windmill.

Someone lit the windmill on fire.

He also keeps drifting from one cluster of people to another. I wish he would stay in one place. I am bad at transitioning to different clusters and tend to orbit two or three familiar configurations. I wish he would stay where I am.

His name tonight is Marie Curie.

I see him in the kitchen. He is with a group of people near the sink. One of the people is the giant anaconda that someone invited. The anaconda makes me nervous, but I approach anyway.

"Yeah," I say, "I did some fucked up shit once."

They all roar approval of my remark.

The anaconda eats someone.

Marie Curie seems glad to see me. We make eye contact for longer than is normal. He says something. He folds a napkin into a wedding dress. I take the wedding dress and wear it on my finger.

I want to kill everyone else at the party so that it is just me and Marie Curie, and then we will dance.

Instead, the anaconda eats me.

I am so embarrassed that I vomit. Inside the anaconda, I choke and weep and imagine the things that people outside the anaconda must be saying about me. The wedding dress on my finger has a hole in it.

Please, Marie Curie, unzip the anaconda like a sleeping bag and climb in with me. Cuddle with me in my vomit.

But that is not what Marie Curie does.

Instead of unzipping the anaconda like a sleeping bag, Marie Curie climbs in through its anus.

And instead of cuddling in my vomit, we cuddle in his.

He says, "I hate the ceiling."

"Why?" The ceiling is ribs and anaconda meat. A chandelier made of paper hangs next to a piñata made of glass. Impossible to tell if the chandelier is giving off light or not, but the piñata definitely is, because it is full of fireflies. "I think I like the ceiling."

"I just—want to see the sky."

He gets up, leaving my side. It had to happen eventually.

I get up and look for my miniature wedding dress. I find a frog beneath the bed. The frog is wearing my wedding dress.

"Look," I say, and show Marie Curie.

Marie Curie looks, and the frog jumps onto his face.

He reels back, stumbles around, blinded by the frog. He

knocks over a lamp. "I want to see the sky!" The lamp—never functional anyway—breaks. "The sky! Not a frog belly!"

"That *is* the sky!"

He takes a knife from the dinner table and starts to stab upward into the ceiling, into the anaconda meat between the ribs. Trying to carve a window. The frog hugs his face, its wedding dress disintegrating.

I take a fork from the dinner table and stab Marie Curie in the arm.

His arm flails out and hits the glass piñata full of fireflies. The piñata shatters, and the fireflies go everywhere.

Everything starts to shake.

I think the anaconda is moving.

The floor jolts up and down, as if the anaconda is running on two legs. I fall. Marie Curie falls. On the table, a bottle of champagne falls.

Champagne spews out in a tidal wave.

The flood of champagne sweeps me along. In it, I find a white horse with a green mane. I mount the horse, and together we surf the wave of champagne as it crashes toward an opening.

An exit.

And then we are outside the anaconda. I stop the horse, and we stand there, dripping golden liquid. The burning windmill is before us. The anaconda is peeing on it. That is why the anaconda was running. That is why I am outside now. The anaconda peed me out.

My horse is made of hard plastic.

The anaconda has legs. It was hiding them earlier. It is actually a dinosaur, not an anaconda. It was impersonating an anaconda for the party, because the party is a masquerade.

I came as a knight.

The dinosaur groans. In its urine, fireflies and silverware and wedding rings tumble out and roll away from the burning windmill. Marie Curie tumbles out, the frog still on his face, and lands in the flames.

The dinosaur stomps away, back toward the house, which has burned down. In the ashes of the house, the man in the bra dances with his grandmother. They have killed everyone else at the party.

The dinosaur eats them.

I turn to the burning windmill and see Marie Curie in the flames with the frog on his face. The frog is made of hard plastic.

The fire turns the plastic into glass.

Marie Curie can see the sky.

Instead of at the sky, he looks at me. We make eye contact for longer than is normal. We agree on what we want.

The windmill is a giant, so I attack it. I gallop my horse into it. The fire turns the horse into glass. I leap at Marie Curie.

The dinosaur stumbles past (it has had too much fun) and vomits on the windmill, and in the vomit is a giant wedding ring. The wedding ring lands on me and Marie Curie. The dinosaur, an ordained minister, has accidentally married us. It laughs and time-travels home.

We turn the accident into a dance.

We run in a circle with the circumference of ourselves.

We time-travel home.

aCKNOWLEDGMENTS

Thanks go out to everyone who ever took a chance on publishing anything of mine. Some of those people are: Bradley Sands, Cameron Pierce, Kirsten Alene, Kevin Shamel, G. Arthur Brown, MP Johnson, D. Harlan Wilson.

Thank you to everyone in the Bizarro community. Some of those people are: Rose O'Keefe, Carlton Mellick III, Jeff Burk, Garrett Cook, Karl Fischer, Vince Kramer, Michael Kazepis, Peter Dale, Andrew J. Stone, Andersen Prunty, C.V. Hunt, Laura Lee Bahr, Jim Agpalza, Tiffany Scandal, John Skipp, Sam Richard, Charles Muir, Brendan Vidito, Mykle Hansen, Jeremy Robert Johnson.

Thank you to Maddie Copp, Travis Verhagen, Mark Terry, and Steve Harrell.

Thank you to Mom, Dad, and Brandon.

PUBLICATION CREDITS

The following stories first appeared (some in slightly altered forms and/or under different titles) in the publications listed:

"Serial Killer Fan Fiction": *The Magazine of Bizarro Fiction*, 2013.
"Analysis of the Analysis of the Breakthrough" (as "Beet-Red Lingams Are Legion"): *The Dream People*, 2008.
"James Brown Saves Christmas": *The Strange Edge,* 2013.
"The Fucking Masterpiece": *Zygote in My Coffee*, 2012.
"Forget Me Not, Filet Mignon" : *Bizarro Bizarro: An Anthology,* 2013.
"To Quit the Chameleon Picnic": *Surreal Grotesque*, 2013.
"Art and Science": *Space Squid*, 2014.
"Everyday Struggle": *The Mustache Factor*, 2013.
"How I Met Your Deformed Mother" (as "Romantic Fucking Comedy"): *Bust Down the Door and Eat All the Chickens*, 2011.
"The Suicidal Moose": *Metazen*, 2013.
"The Suicidal Cat": *Tall Tales with Short Cocks Vol. 5*, 2016.
"Self-Contained Underwater Breathing Apparatus": *Bust Down the Door and Eat All the Chickens*, 2007.
"Light Amplification by Stimulated Emission of Radiation": *Surreal Worlds*, 2015.
"Goodfellas": *The Portland Review*, 2013.

"A False and Hollow Word" (as "Flight of the Onomatopoeia"): *Unicorn Knife Fight,* 2010.

"Very Cold, Very Cozy": *Mondo Bizarro: An Anthology,* 2016.

"My Extremely Horrific Childhood" (as "Bacon Lettuce Tomato Face"): *The Magazine of Bizarro Fiction,* 2012.

"Peaches and Cream": *Bizarro Central,* 2013.

"Sign Here, and Here, and Here" (as "The Meat Grinder Showerhead"): *The Strange Edge Magazine,* 2015.

"Double Chin": *Bizarro Central,* 2012.

"The Balloon Artist": *Linguistic Erosion,* 2012.

"Umbrella": *Bizarro Central,* 2012.

Andrew Wayne Adams is an Amerikan-Kanadian writer and artist. His debut novella, *Janitor of Planet Anilingus*, came out in 2012, and a few people read it. He also writes weird erotica under the name of Emma Steele, though he wants to stop. He has been in the military, worked as a bookseller, worked in warehouses, eaten a Belgian waffle in Belgium, parachuted, hugged his mom, gotten into trouble, and worked in a lab growing stem cells. He is currently pursuing a degree in Molecular Biology and Biochemistry and Computer Science and Karate and Advanced Partying.